"Is that a promise?"

Mariella didn't d_____
moving up and c_____he
was glad only the_____ehind
the counter, as Sa_____e
doorknob. Otherw_____ces
almost knocking to_____the stared at his muscular
frame.

She gave him a little wave as he walked out the door.
When he was gone, her gaze morphed back into focus
even as her brain tried to capture the spellbound way
he'd looked at her, as if he was trying to remember
something about her.

She opened the envelope and read the card aloud.

"'Thank you for helping me to forget.'"

The words, written in neat cursive and signed with his
first name only, intrigued and saddened her at the same
time.

Forget about what, she wondered. *And why?*

Mariella set the box down below the counter, next to
her purse. While stowing the card alongside the British
pound in her wallet, she felt fortunate for their chance
meeting, and her heart began to beat more rapidly, as if
affirming her feelings were true.

She realized she'd received a third gift from Sam Kelly,
though he didn't know he was the one responsible.
Simply by being in his presence, the ice of loneliness
encrusted around her heart had begun to thaw.

He'd made her forget, too.

Dear Reader,

Busy lives may leave little time for romance—especially when you're a single mother, like Mariella Vency, my heroine. Gorgeous soccer star Sam Kelly steps into Mariella's world when she least expects it, and she is forced to admit to herself how much she's missed having a man in her life. The question is—does she want him forever and does he want her? That is the beauty…and the tension…of seduction.

I hope you enjoy *Winning Her Holiday Love*. I'd like to thank all my loyal readers for their support over the past seven years. It's been a dream writing for you, and I hope to continue to do so in the years ahead. Stay in touch with me on my website, www.harmonyevans.com.

Blessings,

Harmony

WINNING *Her* HOLIDAY LOVE

Harmony Evans

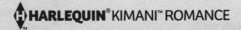
HARLEQUIN® KIMANI™ ROMANCE

Recycling programs
for this product may
not exist in your area.

ISBN-13: 978-1-335-21692-2

Winning Her Holiday Love

Copyright © 2018 by Jennifer Jackson

For questions and comments about the quality of this book please contact us at CustomerService@Harlequin.com.

♦ HARLEQUIN®
™ www.Harlequin.com

Printed in U.S.A.

Harmony Evans received the 2013 Romance Slam Jam EMMA Award for Debut Author of the Year. Her first book, *Lesson in Romance*, garnered two RT Reviewers' Choice Best Book Award nominations in 2012. She currently resides in New York City. Visit her at www.harmonyevans.com.

Books by Harmony Evans

Harlequin Kimani Romance

Lesson in Romance
Stealing Kisses
Loving Laney
When Morning Comes
Winning Her Love
Winning the Doctor
Winning Her Heart

Chapter 1

Mariella cast an eye toward a clock on the wall as she waited for Terrence Jones, the owner of the Beach Bottom Gift Shop, to return from running an errand. She leaned her elbow on the counter and jabbed at a stuffed Santa with her manicured fingernail.

She had been in the midst of shopping for some gag gifts for the office holiday party when he asked her to mind the store. She'd almost said no but the twenty-five percent discount he offered had appealed to her thrifty nature, and would help her win points with her boss.

A former police detective and notorious flirt, Terrence had gotten tired of the rough streets of South Side Chicago and had retired to Bay Point where he peddled trinkets to tourists and residents. Glancing around, she had to give the man some credit. October had just rolled into November and the small shop was already decorated and stocked for the holidays. Terrence had no taste, but at least he had a ton of inventory. She didn't mind doing him a favor but hoped he would hurry back.

Josh, her son, had the day off from school due to a teacher's conference, so she'd taken one, too. Shopping with him always left her with a headache. Getting it done in the early afternoon would help her avoid ruining her entire evening.

Her only child was a senior in high school, a soccer fanatic and a trend follower. Like most teenagers, he always wanted to be seen in the latest styles. The past few months had been rough for Josh, so she tried to do whatever she could to make things easier.

At least the store is empty.

A little unusual, she supposed, for midday during a workweek in downtown Bay Point. As a single mother, she'd learned to be thankful for any time alone, however brief, and wherever it occurred. The downside was she tended to dwell too much on the past.

Mariella reached up and massaged away the tension settling at the back of her neck. However long it took Terrence to get back, she was going to make the best of the situation.

Just like she'd done with Josh.

Raising a son without a father was hard, but she had no choice. Jamaal passed away when Josh was just three years old. He was the love of her life, and although they'd married young, Mariella never regretted it.

At the reading of his will, she'd been shocked to learn he'd inherited a small home on the outskirts of town from his late paternal grandmother. It was the only thing Jamaal had ever owned, and he'd kept it a secret from her. His lawyer told her that he'd dreamed of someday living in it, but sadly, never got the chance.

Three years ago, when Josh was fourteen, they'd moved from East Los Angeles to Bay Point. She wanted a better life for her son, who was starting to hang around the wrong crowd at school.

The small, friendly community welcomed them with open arms. She and her son felt safe, and Josh had thrived in his new school, despite what he felt was "a ton of homework." Although he missed his friends, he quickly made new ones.

After a few months she landed a position as executive assistant to the mayor. The pay was decent and her boss, Gregory Langston, was revered. His family was one of the most powerful in town, and he'd achieved more at his young age than most men did in a lifetime.

At the age of twenty-six, Gregory had become the youngest and the first African-American mayor in Bay Point. Now at age thirty-two, he was well into his second term, happily married to Vanessa, owner of Blooms in Paradise, a local floral shop, and a proud parent of a two-year-old girl.

Due to his efforts, and many others', Bay Point was slowly changing, from boarded-up shops and minimal dining choices to a thriving Northern California tourist destination. New stores, restaurants and housing were popping up everywhere, breathing new life into the old town.

Though she was grateful for her job, it wasn't as challenging anymore. She'd recently finished her bachelor's degree in economics, with a minor in public policy, and desired a role where she could really make a difference.

She balanced her chin on the heel of her palm. Her future had never been so uncertain. She was thirty-four years old and a widow on the brink of being an empty-nester. If a more suitable job opportunity didn't open up in Bay Point, there would be little reason to stay. The mere thought of starting over in a new place made her feel ill.

Being alone didn't necessarily scare her. Though she'd gone out with a few men, the experiences did not go well.

Her child had always been her first priority, and would continue to be even when he was out of the house. Still she couldn't deny that she missed being in a relationship.

Night after restless night she wrestled with her negative thoughts and pent-up desires. Flipping the pillow over to the cold side never helped. Perhaps a man by her side would.

Forcing a smile, and desperate for something to do, she walked over to the back corner of the store. Terrence stored his cleaning supplies in a small cabinet behind a couple of squat, fake palm trees with thick trunks wound with strands of red and green lights.

She rooted around for a dust cloth, and heard the front door creak open. The glass rattled as it closed. Turning, she stayed crouched down, out of sight.

Terrence didn't believe in security cameras, and claimed all he needed were those two palm trees. He'd caught a couple of shoplifters by hiding behind them. She did have a full view of the store, and the customer who had just walked in. She held her breath, recognizing him immediately from the posters that hung in her son's room.

Sam Kelly.

He was one of Josh's favorite professional European soccer players, though her mind blanked on the name of his team. Wherever he was from, he was a long way from home.

Though she was confident he couldn't see her behind the fake foliage, she tucked herself in and against the wall. Her yoga practice, which kept her body toned and limber, was paying off.

"Hello? Anybody here?"

Mariella's heart started to race, like it was doing backflips in reverse, and she couldn't speak. Sam's voice had a dignified, majestic quality to it, classy with an edge of curiosity.

Whoa. This is better than any discount. It wasn't every day she got to spy on a gorgeous man with a British accent.

When nobody answered, he shrugged and began to browse around, hands clasped behind his back.

She'd never scrutinized Sam's glossy image hanging on her son's wall. But now that the sports star was here, right before her eyes, she couldn't help herself.

Sam's toffee-colored skin had the burnished, healthy tinge of someone who spent a lot of time outdoors. She didn't know his age, but surmised he was in his early thirties. He was of above-average height, with the lean, muscular build expected of a professional athlete.

Though it was rude not to make her presence known right away, she wanted to play the voyeur, if only for a moment.

His canary-yellow T-shirt had a slight sheen to it, with a blue coat of arms logo. The black athletic shorts he wore were loose around his muscular thighs, just skimming his knees. The expensive sneakers on his feet, black with gold stripes, were the same ones Josh had begged her to purchase for weeks.

Suddenly, her eyes began to water, and a tickling sensation in her nose followed. She sneezed, just once, quietly as she could manage.

He whirled around. "Who's there?"

She emerged from the palm trees. "May I help you?"

Sam's deep brown eyes glided over her body, drawing pulses of head-to-toe heat, and gleamed a little brighter under the fluorescent lights.

He folded his arms across his chest. "You can tell me what the devil you were doing hiding behind that palm tree."

Being a really awful spy, she thought. The truth embarrassed her, so she decided to make light of the situation and held up two fingers, both shaking slightly. "Actually, it was two palm trees."

A car honked outside, and she nearly jumped out of her skin. Sam acted cool, as if he hadn't heard it. He was probably used to distractions, like thousands of people cheering for him in the stadiums.

"I apologize, but remain confused."

He bowed before her, a gesture that seemed destined for a royal court. It charmed her as much as his posh accent. She wanted to run to the window to see if there was a carriage outside, but suspected there would only be a limousine.

"I was looking for a dust cloth," she explained.

"Behind one, I mean, two palm trees?"

Mariella nodded, despite his dubious tone.

A smile flecked at the corners of his mouth. "What an odd place to keep cleaning supplies."

He shrugged, and then ran a hand over his close-cropped black hair. "Anyway, I'm looking for a holiday gift. Can you help me?"

She let out a breath of relief, thankful he'd changed subjects. "Of course, Mr. Kelly."

"Wait a minute. How do you know my name?"

He took a step toward her, his eyes cautious and his tone guarded.

"My son talks about you all the time. He loves soccer."

She left out any mention of the poster, and that she sometimes watched European soccer on television with Josh. The latter only because she rarely paid attention to the game, preferring to use the time to read a book or shop online.

"Nice to know I have a fan in this town. I was getting a bit worried."

He smiled, more in wonder than in ease, and she couldn't take her eyes off him.

"You're the first person to recognize me."

"Really? Do I get a prize?"

She blushed, not meaning to sound coy or flirtatious, but she was a little surprised at his statement.

Bay Point had begun to rebuild its prior reputation as a destination for celebrities, so it wasn't so unusual he was here. Many of the townspeople were movie and TV buffs. It wasn't inconceivable that some wouldn't be aware of popular sports stars, especially those from overseas.

Sam began to sort through a rack of beach towels. A look of amused horror on his face, he held up one emblazoned with pink and green pineapples.

"I don't know. That depends."

Hope rose within her, but she paused to ensure she answered him with an even tone. "On what?"

"On whether you're a fan of mine, too."

She held back a smile. Was he simply being pretentious? Flirting with her? It was difficult to tell. His overall politeness and good looks could cover a multitude of sins or internal thoughts.

She opened her arms wide.

"I don't know. You just got here."

A smile tipped from his lips right into her heart.

"What's your name?"

She steadied her gaze on his, wondering if she should tell him. If he was just passing through town, she would never see him again.

Sam nudged her elbow playfully as if he sensed her reluctance. "It's only fair, since you already know mine."

"My name is Mariella."

He repeated her name, in a lower voice than before, bringing his accent to a whole new level of sexy. It was as if he was savoring it in his mouth, and an unexpected spark of electricity looped through her body.

"Very pretty."

A knot formed in her throat at his compliment, even though she wasn't sure if he was referring to her name or her looks.

"Thank you," she managed. "Now that we've got the introductions out of the way, I can help you find what you need."

He glanced about the store, in the haphazard way men do when they are overwhelmed by the task of shopping.

"I'm looking for a gift to send back to England."

"For a special girl?"

"Yes. My mum."

His leaned-in, *gotcha*-grin made her cheeks blaze. *Maybe he's single*, she thought, and maybe she should just mind her own business.

"Oh? How sweet." She took a step back, and crashed into a rack of orange bikinis.

Her face heated when one dropped on the floor. She crouched down to pick it up and got an eyeful of Sam's muscular thighs. She was naturally clumsy, so pretending to struggle with the hanger to get a closer look was easy. When she stood, she felt his eyes on her shoulder as she replaced the merchandise to its proper spot.

"Is it her birthday?" she asked, a little light-headed.

She mulled over a rack of maxi dresses emblazoned with colorful beach umbrellas, thinking that might be a nice gift. Considering she lived in Great Britain, which she heard had a lot of rain, she might appreciate a real umbrella instead. Unfortunately, Terrence didn't sell those, so she moved on to a table filled with petrified sea life.

"No. Mum is just a little upset I'm in the States. I need something really nice so she'll know I'm safe, alive and healthy."

Sam picked up a green bejeweled starfish, and shook

his head in disgust. "By the way, the more tasteful and expensive it is, the more it will keep her off my back."

Mariella worried her lip, concerned that due to Terrence's gaudy inventory, she wouldn't be able to help Sam find the perfect gift.

"In that case, I'm not sure if this is the store for you. We cater to tourists who want a special memento of their visit to Bay Point. We may not have what you need."

"I'm sure you have everything I need."

His warm smile and upbeat tone made her almost believe he was talking about her, not something to buy, and reinvigorated her confidence.

"I'm sure I can help you find something." She motioned for him to follow her. "Is she picky?"

"Does the queen live in Buckingham Palace?"

His tone held a note of annoyance, much like Josh's did whenever he felt she was being too overbearing.

Mariella laughed in familiar kinship with the woman, if only because they were both moms of males. She also sensed there was a deeper conflict between Sam and his mother, and suspected his gift would do little to relieve it. How many times had she thought that buying Josh just one more video game would erase the subtle tension between them?

"There are no castles in Bay Point, and while we do have some tacky tourist shops, I can assure you this is a lovely town."

"I'm sure it is, but I'm not here for a visit. I'm the new boys' head soccer coach at the high school. I'm taking over for Coach Lander."

Mariella stopped, her hand poised over a plastic paperweight in the shape of a whale, and blinked in disbelief. News traveled fast in Bay Point and she was surprised she hadn't heard of his arrival.

"I know Coach Lander had a heart attack just before school started in September. Lots of parents were wondering who was going to replace him, but as far as we knew, the administration was still looking."

She handed the object to him, and his smile turned tentative. Somehow she knew it wasn't the whale's fault.

He shrugged and set it back on the display table. "I'm your man, but only until Coach Lander is ready to return full-time. The press release goes out tomorrow."

Though she sensed Sam's discomfort, she couldn't deny her own excitement that he was going to be a temporary resident of Bay Point. Her fingers played with the ends of her hair, and when she caught him looking at her, she stopped.

"My son Josh will be thrilled. He's a forward on the team. Our last name is Vency."

Sam gave her a matter-of-fact nod. "Sounds familiar. Coach mentioned a few kids I should be aware of this season. Your son was on the list."

"How kind." Mariella's heart burst with pride that in the next beat constricted into worry. "I should let you know that Josh did have a bicycle accident this summer, but he's doing okay now."

Sam frowned, and she wondered if she should have mentioned Josh's injury at all. "Was he badly hurt?"

"Yes." She swallowed hard, remembering the aftermath of his accident. "He was on his way home from visiting a friend, and a car sideswiped him. Thankfully, he was wearing a helmet. Still, he landed on his knee."

Sam's eyes crinkled as if he'd just imagined the scene. "Ouch."

Mariella nodded. "He's healed up and his doctor cleared him to play sports, with the caveat that he goes to physical therapy for at least another month."

Recovery over the summer was slow, but only because Josh refused to do his exercises on a consistent basis as instructed by his therapist. Hounding only annoyed him, and frustrated her.

"I'm glad. Coach told me Josh always does his best to put the ball into the net, and he's the key to a winning season this year. He's still going to try out for the team, right?"

Mariella tucked a strand of hair behind her ear. "I'm not sure. It's really up to him."

His amiable smile chased her worry away, but then her fear of Josh playing soccer ratcheted up again, in spite of his handsome, courteous coach. Soccer was a grueling and intense sport, and even though he'd suffered only minor injuries over the past three seasons, that didn't mean he wouldn't get hurt worse.

Still, there was a chance he wouldn't play at all. Ever since the accident, Josh had been sullen and withdrawn. Whenever she mentioned the tryouts or playing soccer again, he changed the subject, or didn't answer her at all. Though he continued to watch soccer on television, she was concerned he'd lost his drive to participate on his former team.

She'd spoken to his doctor about her concerns, and he assured her that things would get better once he got back on the field. Maybe Sam would be able to reinvigorate his enthusiasm and help put her own fears to rest—for good.

"If he doesn't show up, I just may have to recruit you," Sam warned.

Though he probably wasn't serious, the slow grin on his face scored major points with her heart.

"I can run, but I can't kick a ball at all and my aim is terrible," she protested, playing along.

"It's easy. I'll teach you someday."

Whether he was serious or not, a smattering of tingles

flirted through her body and caught her off guard. She tried to laugh them away.

"Thanks. But why don't we find your mother a gift first?"

Mariella wanted to know more about Sam Kelly, but didn't dare ask. He was here, but not to stay, and it was naive to think that what she felt for him now was anything but idle fascination. She wasn't the type to get stars in her eyes, and vowed to keep her senses in check.

That lasted about thirty seconds, and she found herself appraising him again as they weaved their way through the display tables. His upper torso reminded her of a sculpture; the bold angles of his muscles were apparent despite the unfortunate presence of his shirt.

She stood as close as she dared, and the mild waft of musky cologne emanating from his skin drove her crazy. She wanted to snuggle against him and just inhale him first. Other things could come later, she thought wickedly.

Over the next twenty minutes she showed him various items, each of which he dismissed as tacky or cheap, and she silently agreed with his opinions. Despite Sam's sports star status and gorgeous looks, she found herself growing more at ease in his presence. He seemed to be a genuinely nice person, and who wouldn't like a guy who wanted to reassure his mom with the perfect gift?

After perusing every table and display, they ended up near the fake palm trees. She was about to give up when her eye caught sight of a large snow globe. It was perched on the lowest shelf on the wall, very close to where she'd been hiding.

Mariella reached past him, and her arm briefly rubbed against his side. She felt the hairs on her arms stand up as she stooped down to grab it.

She stood and held the snow globe in front of her to examine it more closely. The clear glass bloated the angles of Sam's facial features outward, as if he was standing in front of a fun-house mirror, and she fought back a grin.

"What's so funny?" he asked.

Mariella smiled, surprised he'd noticed her reaction, and rapped on the globe lightly with her knuckles. "I can't believe it's not plastic, like nearly everything else in this store."

He reached for it, but she held it away from him. It was about the size of a grapefruit, and when she flipped it around, the snow inside began to drift over the scene.

The effect was quite charming, and despite the air-conditioning blasting overhead, made her feel warm inside.

"The mountains and the little town below them remind me of Christmas."

As she handed it to him, his fingers grazed hers, and she shivered involuntarily.

"Cold?" he asked, his gaze rimmed with concern.

Mariella shook her head, and rubbed her hands across her upper arms, wishing it were his touch instead. He watched her closely, and by the gleam in his eyes, there was no doubt in her mind he felt something, too.

He held the snow globe up. "I didn't see any mountains on the drive from the airport, so I gather this is not Bay Point?"

"Lord, no. It never snows here," she laughed. "Those are probably supposed to be the Sierra Nevada Mountains, which are north from here. Great skiing, if you're into that sort of thing."

Sam's laughter filled the room, but there was a harsh edge to it, too. "I can injure myself just fine on the soccer field, thank you very much."

"So what do you think?" she asked after he handed it back to her.

"The snow and the mountains will remind my mum of the French Alps. It's perfect. I'll take it." He added a quick wink as if they were partners in crime. "Plus, she knows I hate skiing."

When they got to the counter, Sam held up his phone. "Can I pay with this?"

Mariella shook her head as she rang up his item on the old-fashioned cash register. "As you can see, Terrence isn't that technically advanced."

"You know how to work that thing?"

"A dying talent, I know." She giggled. "When I first moved to Bay Point, I worked here for a few months until I found a full-time job."

Sam slid a bill across the glass. "Okay, this should cover it."

She stared, openmouthed, at it. "Um. We don't take this currency, but we do take credit cards."

Sam palmed his forehead. "I'm sorry. I do have American money."

He thumbed through the cash in his wallet, and handed her a twenty-dollar US bill.

Mariella handed him the correct change, but when she tried to give him the fifty-pound note back, he nudged her hand away and winked.

"Keep it, so I don't accidentally try to use it again and embarrass myself. I'm new in town and want to protect my reputation."

Staring hard at the bill, she wondered if she should accept it and if she did, what it would mean. Possessing something of Sam's made him all the more real in her heart, and that might not be a good thing. But when she looked into his eyes, she could tell right away he was being genuine.

"Thank you, Sam."

She reached under the counter where her purse was

stored and slipped the bill into her wallet, hoping she wasn't making a royal mistake.

"Are you homesick?"

He paused before answering. "Not really. I'm used to traveling and being on the road. This is one of the rare times in my life where I'll be staying put in one place. At least until the soccer season ends."

Their eyes met and held, sending another ray of hope through her mind. It was hard to focus on him while the meaning of his words spun through her brain.

Sam wasn't leaving tomorrow, or the next day, but someday he *would* leave. As far as romance, she had to discard any hint of possibility and keep her heart firmly rooted in reality.

"Shall I gift wrap this for you?"

"Yes, please."

Mariella handed him a pen and a gift tag. While he was writing, she folded a small white cardboard box and gave the inside a generous padding of bubble wrap. After securing the snow globe in white tissue paper, she placed it in the box and taped it shut. Glossy silver wrapping paper and a red bow were the finishing touches.

"Beautifully done, thank you." He slid the tag into an envelope, and she watched as he licked it. "But I'm afraid I've changed my mind."

"What's wrong?" She hitched in a breath and stared at the box, wondering what could have happened.

He placed the envelope on the counter. "I don't think my mother will like this gift after all."

Her eyes snapped to his face. "Why not?"

"I think you'll appreciate it more."

A smile started at the corners of her mouth, even though she was thoroughly confused. She tried to give him the box, but he lifted it away and set it back on the counter.

Her voice trembled. "I don't understand."

"I saw how your eyes lit up when you were looking at the snow globe." He touched her hand and a hot blush slid over her face. "I want you to have it."

He picked up the box and gave it to her, and even though she felt a bit silly, she took it.

"But what about your mom?"

"Is there an antiques store in town?"

She wedged the box under her arm. "Yes, just make a right at the corner and go down a couple blocks. You can't miss it."

"Thanks. I'm sure I'll find something there. Mum loves anything older than her. And since she's perpetually thirty-five, that gives me a lot of leeway."

Sam turned, but seemed reluctant to leave. "I'll let you know what I find the next time I see you."

She smiled, throwing reality aside to ride the seesaw of hope inside her. "Yes. At tryouts."

He backpedaled down the store's center aisle, keeping his eyes on hers the entire way.

"Is that a promise?"

Mariella didn't dare speak, so she nodded, her head moving up and down, seemingly in slow motion. She was glad only the top half of her body was visible behind the counter, as Sam reached behind him to grasp the doorknob. Otherwise, he would have seen her knees almost knocking together as she stared at his muscular frame.

She gave him a little wave as he walked out the door. When he was gone, her gaze morphed back into focus even as her brain tried to capture the spellbound way he'd looked at her as if he was trying to remember something about her.

She opened the envelope and read the card aloud.

"Thank you for helping me to forget."

The words, written in neat cursive, and signed with his first name only, intrigued and saddened her at the same time.

Forget about what, she wondered. *And why?*

Mariella set the box down below the counter, next to her purse. While stowing the card alongside the British pound in her wallet, she felt fortunate for their chance meeting and her heart began to beat more rapidly, as if affirming her feelings were true.

She realized she'd received a third gift from Sam Kelly, though he didn't know he was the one responsible. Simply by being in his presence, the ice of loneliness encrusted around her heart had begun to thaw.

He'd made her forget, too.

Sam stepped outside, closed the door to the shop and squinted. The sun seemed to shine brighter here in California, like it had something to prove to the entire world. Or maybe it was because he'd just met a beautiful woman.

Right now he was glad to be standing on a street corner in Bay Point, rather than in his lonely flat in the south of London. Though a cold shower would be immensely helpful right about now. He'd been hard almost the entire time he was in the store.

He resisted the urge to turn back to look through the window to see if Mariella was watching him. Instead, Sam looked down and exhaled a sigh of relief.

His long soccer shirt and baggy shorts had done their job and hidden his physical reaction to Mariella. As soon as he'd laid his eyes on her, it had sprung to new life.

She wasn't a classic beauty, but had high cheekbones and perfectly arched brows. Thankfully, she didn't possess the haughty cater-to-me manner he'd experienced with many attractive women. Her nut-brown face was clear, smooth, appearing supple to the touch, if he had dared to reach out. Now he wished with every fiber of his being that he had.

Like most men, his lower half acted independently, giving uninvited props to his visual mind and vivid imagination. The sudden and achingly raw desire for her had surprised him.

After a deep, steadying breath, he started to walk in the direction of the antiques store. Out of Mariella's realm, his body began to settle down. Later on, when he was alone, he knew he'd have to contend with images of making love to her.

Sam had broken two of his own unwritten rules for dealing with the opposite sex. First, not to get so enamored with a woman that he lost his senses. Second, never, ever give presents.

Both had happened today, but only one thing would keep him in check. Mariella was the mother of one of his team members, so dating her was out of the question. In fact, it was a stipulation of his contract. And right now he had no desire to travel thousands of miles home. He'd only arrived a few days ago.

His weather app displayed a temperature of sixty-five, yet the sun cresting overhead made it feel much warmer. The heat seemed to radiate from within his body outward, like the longing he'd had for Mariella whenever she got too close.

I wouldn't have minded getting closer.

He sighed again, looked up and shaded his eyes.

Sam heard that it never rained in Southern California, and he hoped the same was true here in the northern region of the state.

He'd come to Bay Point to escape the dreariness of London, and for a lot of other reasons, too, none of which included finding love. Opportunities for sex, on the other hand, seemed to find him, no matter where he was.

Not sure if that was because he was famous or just too damn lucky. He stopped walking, shrugged and kept going. Not really caring.

Except for one woman.

Mariella's interest in him was cool at first. Her guarded actions made it easy to believe she didn't know him. But even before he told her his name, he'd seen the spark in her eyes, when she peeked her head out from behind those ridiculous palm trees.

Their mutual attraction seemed to be as much of a surprise to her as it was to him. As the moments between them went on, it spiraled outward in intensity, like ripples on a pond. The fact that she didn't throw herself at him like so many women did had turned him on even more, though he wished she had.

It became increasingly hard to think straight without seeing her, and wanting her, in his arms. And he knew he was sunk, a rock to her depths.

Every time Mariella moved, it took everything in his power to hold back his steps, to not go to her side right away, and see what she wanted to show him. If he appeared to be a snob, he certainly didn't mean it, even though he did think the merchandise was disposable.

He chuckled to himself, knowing his mother would have called what he felt in his gut a stomachache. Mariella's interest in him? Mere female curiosity.

His mother was very practical, and had neither patience, nor time, for romance. It was a badge of honor that she'd not seen one episode of *Downton Abbey*, although she did say once that she cried when Princess Diana and Prince Charles divorced.

He'd never thought he was the romantic type, either,

and was still puzzled why he'd decided to give Mariella the snow globe. Maybe it was to stop the feelings he didn't understand that made him rock-hard. Thoughts that could only get him into trouble.

At first he thought she'd be angry with him. She'd taken the trouble to wrap the gift so expertly. Would she have taken that much care if she knew it was for herself?

Mixed in with an abject shock was also a grand sense that what he'd done had pleased her.

Her green eyes, set a little too close to her nose, had lit up, but not the same as before. Rimmed with the darkest, longest lashes he'd ever seen, her eyes had shone like gentle beacons, guiding him somewhere he'd never been before. If he dove into their depths, what would he find? What would she?

Pushing his thoughts aside, he continued on Ocean Avenue, Bay Point's version of Main Street. With its copper streetlamps, the blue-green patina reminiscent of the ocean, and the cracked, sand-dusted sidewalks, the little town had undeniable signs of stubborn longevity. He passed Bay Point Bed-and-Breakfast, his temporary lodging, owned by Maisie Barnell. She was a nice woman, if not a little nosy, who loved to carry on a conversation. For hours on end, it seemed. The sooner he found a more suitable place to live, the happier he'd be.

On his way to the antiques shop, he peeked into storefronts and caught a bit of shade now and again under their colorful cloth awnings. Many of the merchants were taking advantage of the weather to begin their holiday decorating. He dodged ladders draped with strings of lights and boxes of pine boughs and wreaths.

Sometimes he forgot to walk in the practiced manner that helped hide his slight limp, although the residual pain from his injuries was gone for the time being. His mind seemed stuck on Mariella, like a bolt stripped of its grooves, and though he knew it was wrong, he couldn't wait to see her again.

He thought of how her cowl-necked ivory blouse, the fabric sheer enough to trick the eye, hinted at the fullness of her breasts. Tonight he'd be dreaming about the way her navy skirt clung to the curves of her torso, and wake up wishing he was kissing her head to toe.

But it was her smile that had struck him the most. It was worth the stress of shopping, an activity that he despised, made worse because it was a gift for his mother.

When he'd hinted to Mariella that he would recruit her for his team, her full mouth had drawn together in a lush bow of shock, but almost immediately after, the right corner of her lip had smarted, as if she was intrigued, though it could have been a nervous tic.

The silent respect she appeared to have toward him, and what was underneath her reserved and cautious nature just waiting to be discovered, excited him, too. He didn't readily understand his feelings, but for the time being, he accepted them at face value.

Mariella was a woman he could chase, if he decided to, rather than someone chasing him, as per usual.

Was she single?

She wore no ring, but that didn't mean she didn't have a husband, boyfriend or lover. A band of gold or a glittery diamond only meant as much as two people ascribed to it. He'd never knowingly broken up a relationship, but he did believe in fate.

It was a shame she was off-limits.

Sam found the antiques shop, but it was closed. There was an Apartment For Rent sign in the window. After putting the number into his phone, he walked on until he reached a small café. He ignored the signs hawking peppermint lattes and bought an iced tea with lemon. The drink was refreshing, but did not cool his yearning for Mariella.

After he was done, he double-backed toward the inn. He had an early evening meeting with his assistant coaches that should help him focus on what was important.

A man in a pink-and-tan Hawaiian shirt hurried toward him down the narrow sidewalk, carrying a paper sack. Sam stepped aside to let him pass, but the guy nearly collided into him anyway.

The old Sam would have gotten upset at the man's rudeness; not enough to say anything mean, however, the incident alone would have pricked at him all day.

But ever since his devastating injury, he tried not to get too upset or angry anymore, especially over things in life he couldn't control. His mind was too busy, trying to reason, trying to process all the possible outcomes for his future. Like whether he would ever return to pro soccer, or even the United Kingdom, for that matter.

The *what-ifs*.

The *what-now*.

Everything in his life had changed, including him.

While he'd failed to find an appropriate gift for his mother, he might have found the perfect woman. Sam smiled with the realization that his time in the United States, however brief, could prove to be interesting and satisfying.

He knew better than anyone that there were always multiple ways to a goal.

Chapter 2

"Josh! Come on! We've got to go now or we'll be late!"

"I told you," Josh yelled back. "I don't want to go!"

He had just turned seventeen in September and his voice sounded as deep as a man's. But in Mariella's heart, he was still her little boy.

His father was six foot two, but Josh rang out at five foot eight inches, and he was still growing.

His upper body was compact and ripped with muscles. There was a full-length mirror in the mudroom, which she'd installed so she could double-check her appearance before she went outside. Sometimes she caught him looking at his reflection and she hoped he liked what he saw. He was such a handsome young man.

Josh was also a gifted athlete, and his greatest strength lay in his legs. His speed and grace on the field had helped the Bay Point Titans become one of the best high school soccer teams in the NorCal region.

She leaned against the stair railing and took out a cloth-covered band from the back pocket of her running shorts. Gathering up her long, black hair into a neat ponytail, she tapped her foot on the bare wood floor and considered her options.

Going upstairs to continue the conversation would likely result in an argument. Lord knows there were plenty of those recently. But allowing Josh to continue to stew in self-pity was not going to help him get out of the funk he'd been in since the accident.

No matter his age, she would never stop worrying that he would get hurt. She also wouldn't allow him to quit the team out of self-pity. If he didn't show up at tryouts that was essentially what he was doing.

Her heart blossomed with renewed hope that getting him back on the soccer field where he belonged would help make everything right again.

Especially between us.

They'd been so close, prior to moving to Bay Point. For a long time, Josh was angry with her for taking him away from his friends, some of which he'd known since kindergarten. Though he'd eventually settled in and made plenty of new ones, he never let her forget how much he missed his "real" home.

Wearily, Mariella started to climb the narrow stairs, which always felt like Mt. Everest whenever she had to try to get Josh out of his room. To take her mind off the conflict that lay ahead, she ran her fingertips lightly against the mauve wallpaper, original to the Colonial-style house. It was worn, but the silk-like texture still felt luxurious.

She could have replaced it, and a lot of other things in the house by now, but something always stopped her. Redecorating was time-consuming and expensive, but it also meant setting down permanent roots.

She'd learned a long time ago to look for the beauty in life, which she often found in the oddest of places. It was easier than trying to understand life itself, and required no real commitment on her part.

Soon, though, it would be time to decorate for the holidays, something she did enjoy doing, and she made a mental note to have Josh start bringing all the holiday decorations down from the attic.

They usually went back home to South Central LA to visit her parents for Thanksgiving. Before they left, Mariella would have the tree and everything else up, so that when she got back, she could just enjoy the holidays.

She took a deep breath before stepping into Josh's room, and held back a frown. He was playing computer games as usual. Headset over his ears, palm over his mouse, he wore an old Bay Point Titans T-shirt and shorts. A good sign. At least he was thinking about going to tryouts.

The blinds were shut, but the windows were open and a mild breeze blew in fresh air, overriding the subtle odor of dirty socks, corn chips and wet towels.

Mariella pursed her lips in mild annoyance. A few slats were broken on one of the blinds. She'd warned Josh to be careful raising and lowering them. They, too, were original to the house, and were fragile due to age.

It was obvious he hadn't listened to her, but she decided to let it go. The argument wasn't worth it. The house she'd inherited had already proven to be a money trap and she made another mental note. Add blinds to the list of things in the house needing to be repaired, besides their relationship.

Mariella turned the wand, allowing the morning sunlight to stream into the room. The warm rays spreading over her face helped wash away her irritation.

Josh turned in his chair and lifted his arm over his eyes. "What did you do that for?"

"To see if you would melt," she replied with a smile.

"Ha-ha." His arm thumped back against his desk and he didn't bother to look up at her.

As Mariella stepped toward him, her foot nudged an empty water bottle. She picked it up and wedged it under her armpit.

"What's not funny is the fact if we don't leave soon you will miss your opportunity to play soccer this year."

"So?" he muttered, eyes focused on the screen.

"So...it's your senior year," Mariella responded sternly, ignoring his insolent tone. "This is your last chance to letter in the sport, which as you know, looks—"

"Great on my college applications and could help me get a scholarship," he replied impatiently. "I know, Mom. You've told me this a million times."

She snapped her fingers. "Then if you know, let's get going."

Josh fiddled with his headset and Mariella hoped their conversation wasn't being broadcast throughout the internet.

"I told you before. I don't ever want to play soccer again. And even if I did, I can't. Not like before. Not with my knee."

His voice cracked a little, and her heart broke a little more for the pain he'd suffered over the past several months.

Mariella softened. "I understand you're—" she stopped herself from using the word *afraid* "—concerned, but the doctor cleared you for sports. Though it may feel uncomfortable at first, you're okay to play."

His lips trembled, but he still refused to look at her and continued to focus his attention on some sort of military-looking game. From her brief glance at the screen, it had everything she hated—guns, blood and gore.

"I don't care. Besides, Coach Lander isn't even going to be there."

"No, but Sam Kelly is, remember? You were so excited when I first told you he was stepping in to coach the team. What happened?"

Josh jerked his chin toward her, his tone abrasive. "I still think he's cool, all right? At least the administration didn't replace him with some chump who doesn't know anything. Or worse, a parent."

"Good deal. No chumps, no parents. You'll be fine."

"No, I won't," he insisted. "Coach Kelly is a pro player, so he'll probably want me to be perfect. He'll want everyone on the team to be as good a player as he is."

"I'm sure he just wants you to try your best."

"With this knee?" he snorted, returning his attention to the computer.

She put her hand on his shoulder, which he promptly shrugged off. "You're cleared medically, Josh. And you're still taking physical therapy, so if there is any soreness after practices, we can get it taken care of right away."

His hand paused over the mouse, and she could almost see his brain whirring.

"If I go, will you puh-leeze lay off me?"

Mariella hesitated. She didn't want him to try out to get her off his back. She wanted him to go because he wanted to play soccer, but she had to start somewhere.

"Maybe. But only because you said please."

He rolled his eyes, and Mariella held in a sigh of relief as he slipped on and laced up his soccer cleats.

When Josh stood, she exhaled and gave him a hug.

"Do me a favor. Don't give up before you even get on the field."

He broke away quickly, and she blinked back the start of tears. She tried not to let it bug her when he resisted her affection, but it did.

"I won't have to even bother trying. The coach will take one look at me and give up for me."

She set her lips in a firm line. *He better not.*

The thought of anyone not doing right by her son made her temples pulse with anger and the beginnings of a headache sprout.

She was concerned about Josh. He continued to blame himself for the bike accident, even though it wasn't his fault. Worse, he never wanted to talk about his feelings; instead, his behavior and attitude spoke for him.

Would things have been different if his father were alive? It was a question always in the back of her mind.

With her heart in her throat, Mariella followed her son as he walked slowly down the stairs.

On the way to the high school, Mariella racked her brain trying to think of something to say that wouldn't upset Josh. The drive was short, but the silence between them made the time drag, and knots formed in her stomach.

Seeing Sam again made her both nervous and excited. Since the article about his new position dropped in the *Bay Point Courier*, the whole town was abuzz. The town had a colorful history as a secret hideaway for movie stars, but this was the first time a well-known sports figure had made his way to its sandy shore. And he hailed from London, no less, home of kings, queens and princesses.

She wondered if the man had had any privacy since.

Mariella stole a glance at Josh. He seemed lost in thought, and likely hoped he wouldn't have to talk at all. As soon as she parked, he grabbed a water bottle and his gear, and with an emotionless "see ya," strode off.

At least he said goodbye, she thought, watching him slowly half jog, half walk toward the field.

He's going to be okay, she told herself for what seemed like the millionth time. *And so will I.*

She reached the bleachers, sat down and scanned the field.

Sam hadn't arrived yet, so she eyed the track surrounding the perimeter, aiming to get in the miles she'd missed in the morning. One of the elementary schools was in dire need of a new playground, but there were no funds in the local budget, so she was working with the board of education to write the application for a state grant. She'd volunteered her skills and time, hoping the experience would help further her career.

Mariella stood, turned and put one foot on the bleacher and began to retie the laces of her worn running shoes.

Suddenly, she looked up and cringed at the metallic twang caused by two children bounding down the stairs, and at the sight of Leslie Watkins trailing behind them. Her son, Dante, was one of Bay Point High School's star athletes, and she let everyone in town know it.

She was thinking so hard about Josh and Sam she hadn't seen Leslie, a woman who made it a point to be noticed by everything and everyone.

"I'm so glad tryouts are being held in the morning," Leslie called out, waving her manicured hand in front of her face.

Mariella took her time tying her shoelaces, and then looked up, stifling her annoyance. Conversations with Leslie simply started, without a hello and often without any context, and ended without a goodbye.

"Agreed. It's only ten a.m. and I'm sweltering."

Leslie got down to the bottom step and pushed her sunglasses on top of her head.

"You're going to run in this weather?"

Mariella ignored the dumbfounded look on Leslie's face.

Her metabolism was slow, and seemed to decrease every year with age. It was hard work maintaining her curves.

She grinned and patted her flat tummy. "Have to work off a giant lemon bar I ate at Ruby's this morning."

Leslie narrowed her eyes, and Mariella guessed it was her weak attempt to show understanding. "That shop has a lot of us hitting the gym, me included."

Mariella found that hard to believe. Leslie was model-tall and as thin as a birch stick, with the bitchy personality and spray tan to match.

"I guess no one can resist them, even you," Mariella replied as she vowed inwardly to avoid any sweets. That morning's indulgence would have to be the last one for a while. She was starting to train for a half marathon, her first, and it was time to push her body beyond its current limit and control her desires.

Leslie cupped her hands around her mouth. "Matt! Jamie! Don't go any farther than the playground," she yelled, and then turned back to Mariella. "Normally we would stay and watch, but today I'm very, very busy."

"Don't let me keep you," Mariella said lightly, eager to get rid of the woman. She didn't know how long the try-outs would take and she wanted to get her run in.

Plus, she already saw Leslie plenty. She was PTA president and Mariella was vice president, and both were very active in the school.

She grabbed hold of her right ankle, pulling her calf back toward her buttocks to stretch her hamstring. She hoped Leslie would take the hint, but instead she shaded her eyes and prattled on.

"Dante looks good out there, doesn't he?"

"Yes. Both of our boys have grown so quickly. I can't believe they're seniors!"

Mariella spotted Josh kicking a ball toward the white-netted goal. From a distance, he looked as though he couldn't care less if he made it in or not, while Dante was moving so fast his blond crew cut flashed in the sunlight as he passed the ball from one player to another.

Leslie folded her arms and sighed. "Dante turned eighteen earlier this month. We wanted to celebrate in Hawaii, but as usual, we had to postpone until the end of soccer season."

"Oh, really?" she responded, trying to sound interested though she couldn't care less.

Mariella recalled that for Josh's birthday they spent the day at the beach and then went to his favorite restaurant. She couldn't afford Waikiki, and most of her savings was going to his college fund, but at least he hadn't spent all day in his room.

Leslie slipped her sunglasses back over her eyes. In the haze of her dark lenses, Mariella could almost feel a verbal jab coming on, like a nasty cold.

"You look so young to have a teenage son," Leslie said, her tone riddled with vague condescension. "I've been meaning to ask you. What's your secret?"

Mariella clenched her toes in her sneakers, uneasy about the question, even though she'd been asked it by nosy people throughout Josh's life. It was nobody's business then, and it sure as hell wasn't Leslie's business now.

One didn't have to peer close to see the crow's feet at the edges of Leslie's eyes, and Mariella felt blessed to have the type of skin that aged well.

She pasted on a smile and tapped the brim of her baseball cap. "I stay out of the sun."

"In California? Good luck!" Leslie said with a burst of laughter, followed by a dramatic sigh. "Well, I guess the Big Island is still fabulous in March."

Mariella fought the urge to roll her eyes at Leslie's aggrieved tone. At the low sound of sporadic clapping, she lifted her chin and held back a frown as she watched Josh half run, half limp away from the goal.

Leslie followed her gaze. "Are you sure he's ready to play so soon after the accident?" Her voice was almost a whisper as if she was afraid Josh could somehow overhear.

Despite a firm assurance from the doctor, it was the same question Mariella wrestled with day after day, night after night. But she wasn't about to reveal her worries and woes to Leslie.

She forced a smile, as she had so many times in the past few months, in spite of the pain of seeing her son combat his injury.

She had to help him triumph.

"Dr. Hamilton gave him the all-clear."

Leslie lifted her thin nose into the air. "Just because he's the father of the mayor's wife, doesn't mean you have to believe everything the man says. You should get a second opinion."

About to put her Mama Bear gloves on, Mariella bit back a sharp retort that could have had tongues wagging in Bay Point for weeks.

"Josh is fine, Leslie. But thanks for inquiring."

"If you say so," she replied.

She jogged in place, wishing Leslie would just go away, but the woman flashed a conspiratorial grin.

"But I'll tell you who definitely *is* fine…the new soccer coach," she blurted. "If we gals have to suffer in the stands, at least we've got some eye candy this season."

There was no way Mariella was going to tell her she'd already met Sam several days earlier, so she feigned ignorance.

"Oh, yes, I read an article about him in the newspaper."

Leslie waved her comment away. "I knew about him for weeks."

"How did you find out before everyone else?"

She frowned as if she couldn't believe she was asked the question.

"Don't worry about it, Mariella. Unlike that old coot Maisie, I have access to real, legitimate information that matters. Like hot new arrivals to our little town."

Maisie was the unofficial matriarch of Bay Point. People sought her out and told her things because they trusted her to listen. As far as Mariella knew, she always used her information to help, not hurt. She wasn't an "old coot;" she was a valued member of the community.

Mariella's fingers shook with anger as she adjusted the band on her upper arm that held her smartphone.

Maisie was driving home from the grocery store when she witnessed Josh's bike accident and called 911. She also organized meals with her church group and had them delivered to Mariella's home. She would never forget what Maisie had done for her and Josh, and hoped to someday repay the favor.

"I had no idea who he really was," Leslie continued as if Mariella wasn't even there. "I really don't pay attention to the sport." She licked her lips. "But now that I know what he looks like, I sure wish I had."

"Hot new arrivals?" Mariella repeated. She cocked a brow and kicked at a few pebbles with the toe of her right shoe. "Don't forget, you're married to one of the most successful men in town."

"Yes, but that doesn't mean a girl can't look."

Leslie fanned her hand in front of her face. "And, honey, when I look at Sam, mine eyes have seen the glory!"

Mariella held back a smile, watching Leslie act like an

overgrown teenager, and was determined to keep the gaga factor in check.

"We've already had some private conversations," she confided in a tone meant to incite curiosity, but Mariella refused to bite.

Leslie winked as if sharing a secret. "Here comes the man himself, and because I'm your friend, I'll let you have a turn."

She walked away, without saying goodbye, of course.

"You are not my friend," Mariella muttered when she was out of hearing distance. But she wouldn't want her for an enemy, either.

She slid her sunglasses on and turned her attention to Sam. Clad in dark blue shorts and a Titans polo shirt, he could have been a model for a men's fashion magazine. The only clue he was a coach was the whistle hanging around his neck.

He looked good far away, but she knew—and apparently, Leslie did also—he looked even better close up. She shook the thought from her head and watched him approach. He didn't appear to be in too much of a hurry to get to her.

But as she continued to study him, she noticed that while his gait was confident, he did favor his left leg every once in a while. It was as if there was a hiccup in his step.

Growing impatient to see him, she decided to meet him halfway. No use in him thinking that she was an overblown diva like Leslie. Besides, she told herself as she jogged toward the middle of the field, her feet were itching to run away all her stress. About five feet away from him, out of breath, sweat trickling down her spine, with her legs about to collapse in a heap on the ground, she stopped in her tracks. Not because she was out of shape. She wasn't.

It was the way he was looking at her. Even though he

had dark sunglasses on, she could feel a haze of desire emanating from him, and this time, she wasn't afraid.

The sight of Mariella…was a wonder. Better than the first time, yet still as powerful, like an unexpected punch in the gut. A sudden fishhook of attraction made breathing a little harder. The hair on his arms stood up even as he told himself to chill out.

What the hell was wrong with him?

Sam stopped for a few seconds, rolled his shoulders back and continued to walk to her, ignoring the slivers of pain darting through his left leg.

Her body appeared more athletic than he'd first noticed at the shop, probably because it was hidden under her office clothes. He thought about her being nestled against him, and cords of his back muscles furrowed and pulsed.

Today she wore black, body-hugging nylon jogging pants that ended at the ankle, orange-and-black running shoes, a tight fitting camisole top and a baseball cap.

Somehow, he managed to speak.

"Hello, Mariella. It's nice to see you again."

He loved the way her name rolled off his tongue.

He refused to call her Ms. or Mrs. Vency. She could correct him, if she chose. Somehow, he kept his hands planted against his sides, instead of reaching for her trim, little waist.

How easy it would have been to bring her body close to curve against his. If they were alone, and if it wasn't for that darn contract.

Her skin gleamed in the hot sun, making his stomach quiver in an outlandish way, like he was on a roller coaster, click-clacking up a hill, not knowing what was on the other side.

Sam wasn't afraid of heights. *God, no.* He wasn't afraid of anything, except what this woman could mean to him.

He couldn't keep his eyes off her.

Dark sunglasses, the perfect cover. He could have been staring somewhere past her head, centering his attention on some imaginary dot in the distance, instead of the small circle of diamonds that hung on a thin gold chain just above the notch of her cleavage. He wondered who had given her such a sexy necklace.

His curiosity was like an itch he couldn't scratch, much like his need for her. He figured he'd better get used to it. Hoping she couldn't see his desire, and at the same time, wishing she could feel with her own hands how much he wanted her.

"I'm glad you showed up. Now, let me see. What position should I give you?"

His statement was unabridged flirtation, but no one was around. No one could hear. He hadn't even played one game yet, and he was in danger of breaking his contract already.

Sam waited as she crossed her arms, anticipating her reaction. He didn't expect amusement.

"I told you before that I'd make you lose. I told you I'm terrible at sports."

"And I told you I would teach you."

He smiled, hoping to dazzle her, but the look on her face was anything but. It was almost as if he'd gone over the line, and her deep frown was his penalty.

"I'm not important, Coach. But my son is. All I care about is whether or not Josh makes the team."

Sam's heart fell at the slight hardness in her voice. The fact that she'd addressed him so formally didn't escape his attention, either.

He sighed inwardly, and wasn't going to bother to flirt

with her again. Maybe he'd read her wrong. It was clear from her tone he'd better stop while he was ahead, even though he didn't get nearly as far as he wanted to.

"If he works hard, I don't see why not. Tryouts will give me a good perspective."

"I've always thought tryouts were so unnecessary. Why can't those who played last season automatically be considered for the next?"

Now it was his turn to cross his arms, like a boss.

"It's to make sure that the position each guy had last season is still the right one for him, the one he wants to play, and is good for the entire team."

She rubbed her hands together. "I don't know if you've noticed, but Josh…" Her voice trailed off. "Limps a little sometimes. As I mentioned the other day, he was involved in a bike accident and his left knee was injured."

He glanced back over one shoulder. The faces of his players were hard to see, their arms and legs blurred, little meteors of movement across the field.

"Which one is your son?"

Mariella laughed. "I'm sorry. I forgot you've never seen him in person. Josh is the one in the sky-blue shorts, and the Bay Point Titans team shirt, of course."

He turned back. "No, I hadn't noticed his limp. But then again, most of the players just arrived, and I haven't had a chance to evaluate anyone yet."

She sucked in a breath. "You won't hold it against him, will you?"

He ran a thumb across his bottom lip, pausing a beat when he saw Mariella was watching him, looking doubtful.

"Not exactly."

She folded her arms tightly against her chest. "What do you mean, *not exactly*? His doctor cleared him for sports. Surely you'll take into consideration his—"

He held up a hand. "I treat everyone the same. Everyone gets the chance to succeed, or fail."

It was what he wanted for himself, if he ever returned to pro soccer. He didn't want his teammates feeling pity for him, making things easy. If he wasn't ready to put one hundred and fifty percent effort into every game, like he had for almost ten years, then he wasn't fit to be on the team, let alone playing a sport that demanded so much from him.

Mariella pursed her lips, reminding him of how kissable they looked. "I can respect that, just as long as Josh isn't on the bench all season."

"That's up to him. I can't guarantee that he won't be on the bench. After all, it is the only place to sit on the field," he said, trying to lighten the mood. "But if he tries his best, and shows commitment to the team, he'll do fine."

Mariella frowned. "All I'm asking is for you to give my son a fair shot."

"A fair shot?" he repeated. "A second ago you were practically begging for me to go easy on him."

The ponytail on top of her head waved back and forth like a snake.

"I don't want that. Not really. I'm just worried about him, that's all."

He took a chance and put his hand on her shoulder. Touched her just long enough and light enough to verify her skin was as warm and silky-smooth as he'd imagined. Best of all, she let him.

Sam lowered his voice. "I'll take care of him," he assured her, reluctantly pulling his hand away. "No worry lines on that beautiful face, okay?"

The edge of a smile appeared on her lips. "When will you be making your decision?"

"Sometime this week. We've got a game next Saturday, and I'll need his final paperwork before he can play."

"Just send it home with Josh and I'll make sure to sign it."

Mariella started to jog away, but he touched her arm again. She turned around, hands on her hips.

"If he's hurting, he should tell me. I know what it's like."

She looked at him, her eyes softening, but she didn't ask what he meant, didn't ply him with questions.

Smart woman. No wonder he liked her.

Chapter 3

Mariella pulled the stopper and stepped out of the claw-foot tub. She watched the water swirl down the drain and hoped it would take her thoughts of Sam with it.

Seeing him at tryouts confirmed one thing in her mind. The man was either dangerous to her stable life, or the antidote for it.

She was drying off when the doorbell rang. Quickly, she hung up her towel and wrapped herself in her white terry-cloth robe.

Josh had called a little over an hour ago to tell her he was going to have dinner with friends after soccer practice. Maybe he'd changed his mind and decided to hang out with his mom instead, or more likely, his computer.

She tossed a rueful glance back at the vanity, where her homemade carrot and honey mask, and a stack of unread magazines, beckoned to her. Both would have to wait. Her son needed her.

"Josh, did you forget your keys again?" she shouted, padding downstairs in her bare feet.

She peeked through the curtain, and instantly wanted to melt face-first into the door. Instead, she unlocked and opened it wide.

She braced her shoulder against the jamb. "I didn't know coaches made house calls."

Sam had a way of making his standard uniform of long black shorts and a gold-and-blue Bay Point Titans T-shirt look naturally elegant. No whistle hung around his neck, but that was okay, because she was whistling at him in her mind. His skin was darker than when she'd seen him last. The long days spent in the sun made the hair on his arms and legs more obvious.

"And I didn't know you were home. I was looking for Josh. Is he here?"

The smile he gave her was better than the most luxurious bubble bath. It slid around, under and through her, and made her tremble. But the tenor of his voice seemed overly professional, as if he wanted no misinterpretation, and that threw her off guard.

She clutched the top of her robe in her fist. "Oh. Josh told me he was going out with friends after practice."

His eyes passed over her face, then midchest to her hands. "May I come in, anyway?"

She hesitated, remembering the heat that coursed through her body just being near him in the store, and then on the soccer field. Now he was on her front steps, where it would be so easy to throw her arms around his neck, her legs around his hips. Instead, she dropped her hands and waved him inside.

He bowed slightly before entering, and her mouth twitched at his formality. Maybe she could curtsy her way into his heart, she mused as he followed her into the small living room.

"Sorry for the mess in here. As you can see, I'm getting ready to decorate for the holidays."

Two small easy chairs were laden with old magazines and newspapers Mariella had found in the attic during the weekend, including back issues of the *Bay Point Courier*. She was fascinated by the history of the little town, but hadn't read any of them yet.

Most of the weekend was spent digging through the boxes that held all of her decorations. There were sets of ceramic snowmen and snowwomen, Mr. and Mrs. Claus, poseable elves made of green felt, and colorful wooden nutcrackers in various sizes.

Sam weaved around the towers of boxes and joined her. "No problem. I take it you love Christmas?"

"Everything but the credit card bill afterward."

The only other seating option available in the room was an antique love seat. She preferred more modern designs, and was slowly selling everything she didn't like, except this one. It was so small she had no choice but to sit nice and close to Sam.

They sat down on the edge and swiveled toward each other. Their knees bumped, causing the flap of her robe to peel back. Part of her lower left thigh was exposed and she felt a kiss of cold air on her skin.

Mariella considered smoothing the fabric back in place, but didn't want to call attention to something he may not have even noticed. How easy it would be to slip her robe from her shoulders, or allow him to do the honor. He'd notice then. He'd notice everything about her.

"This is cozy."

Mariella smiled. "Henry Wexler calls it a settee. Did you ever get a chance to go into his store?"

"I did. I bought a beautiful antique silver tea set. Mum collects them and hates tea. Go figure." Sam shrugged. "Even better. I'm renting Wexler's upstairs apartment."

She raised a brow. "Oh, I didn't know he owned the entire building."

"Yes. Lucky for me, he had a vacancy, and it's completely furnished. I moved in last weekend."

Mariella didn't have to ask where he lived before. The day after she met him at the store, Maisie was visiting the mayor, and on her way out, she told her that Sam was staying with her. If she hadn't personally met Sam, she would have pressed the woman for more details about him. But since she had, she felt an odd sense of loyalty he really hadn't earned yet.

"I'm glad you're getting settled in. Now, I'm not sure why you are here, but can whatever you have to say wait until I go change into some real clothes?"

"What if I say I like you now, just as you are?"

Her nipples tightened at the sexy lilt of his accent, and when she squirmed in place, they rubbed against the thick fabric of her robe. She wondered what he would do if he could see how his voice affected her, and what it would be like to hear it every day.

Leaning back against the armrest, she looked him straight in the eye. Her robe opened slightly in the middle, revealing the curve of her breast. She left it alone, not caring if he noticed, daring him to stare.

"Let's cut to the chase. Why are you here, Sam?"

Sam folded his hands across his chest, like he wasn't sure what to do or say next, and his eyes slid shut. When he opened them, they were troubled.

"I'm concerned about Josh. He wasn't at practice today."

"What?" Mariella straightened with alarm. "He just called me."

His sympathetic look did not ease her anxiety. She was overjoyed when Josh was accepted to the team in the same position he'd played last season. To learn he wasn't fulfilling his obligations was distressing.

"I'm not saying he didn't. I'm just telling you he didn't call from the field."

"I don't understand. Is this the first practice he's missed?"

Mariella rubbed her hand against her forehead, embarrassed and stressed at the same time. Did raising a teenage son ever get easier?

Sam nodded. "Yes, but he's been distracted at the others. Is everything okay here at home?"

She bristled openly. "What are you saying? Are you accusing me—?"

"Calm down. I just want to help."

He tried to touch her arm, but she inched away, ready with a sharp, practiced retort. "We don't need your help, Sam."

Hurt flashed in his eyes, but her deep indignation refused to acknowledge it. Though he probably meant well, she hated when anyone insinuated that she couldn't handle her own kid.

"Everything's fine." She made a measured effort to soften her tone. "I'm sorry Josh ditched practice. That's not like him at all, but I wonder where he is?"

Sam took his time answering, and she wondered if he thought she was overreacting.

"Probably hanging with friends, just like he told you, so I wouldn't worry. The good news is that he's playing well."

She sighed with relief, even though inside she was only mildly reassured. "I'm glad to hear. By the way, I never got a chance to thank you for admitting him to the team."

Sam shrugged, like he knew all along Josh would make it.

Mariella had hoped that because of her son's injuries, Sam would take it easy on him. On the flip side, she also wanted Sam to treat him equally and fairly. She'd learned the hard way that coddling could be damaging her son's self-esteem, and she blamed herself for their strained relationship.

"He earned it. But remember only he'll know if his playing is affected by his injuries."

Mariella inclined her head toward Sam, knowing he was right. She could only pray that Josh would speak up if he was having problems.

"Do you think that's why he is having trouble focusing?"

"It's possible. If he can identify the issues he's having, I can help him make some adjustments. It's better than just not coming to practice."

Mariella put her hand on her chest, suddenly pained that her son could be running away from his problems, rather than facing them head-on.

"Thanks. I'll tell him, after I ground him for the rest of his life for lying to me," she said with a wry grin.

She rarely punished Josh, which she'd come to realize was part of the problem. Still, a long talk was in order when he came home.

"Glad I could help, but I have another concern I want to speak to you about."

A tickle of worry rose in her stomach as his eyes perused her face. "About Josh?"

He shook his head. "No, the soccer field. It's playable, but in terrible condition. I was wondering if you or any of the other parents had noticed it."

"I did," she affirmed. "But I haven't heard any complaints from the other parents. Did you ask Coach Lander about it?"

"Yes. He felt bad he wasn't around this summer to manage things so the proper maintenance could have been done."

She chuckled softly, but meant no offense. "The guy

does baby it as if it was his own lawn. What are you going to do?"

"We can use sod in some places to fill in the ruts and holes, and lessen the chance for injury. But that's only a temporary fix. What the school really needs is a brand-new field. If the decision was up to me, I would recommend they upgrade to artificial turf."

Mariella raised a brow. "You mean the kind they use for pro football?"

He gave her a slow nod. "And the kind I've played on my entire career. I was thinking about talking to the athletic director about my concerns. Since I'm only a temporary employee, do you think that's out of line?"

"No, not at all. I think that's a great idea." She tapped her index finger on her chin. "Maybe there's a way I can help."

"Really?" Sam leaned forward, sending a pleasant whiff of his cologne her way. "I'm all ears."

She crossed her legs. "I'm the vice president of the Bay Point High Parent-Teacher Association. We help raise money to fill the gap where budgets fall short and advocate for our children within the school system. Do you have an organization like the PTA in the United Kingdom?"

"Maybe. I went to a boarding school, where it was every kid for himself."

She smiled. "I'm not promising anything, but I'll talk to the principal. You handle the athletic director."

Sam gave her a teasing grin. "And maybe we can meet in the middle?"

"We'll see," she replied. Excited about the prospect of teaming up with Sam, it was difficult to keep her voice and emotions on an even keel.

"Thanks. Looks like you and I are going to see a lot more of each other. I've missed you."

Warmth spread through her body, even though he was probably just being polite. After all, everyone on the team would benefit from a new field.

"You did? Why?"

He gave her a sheepish smile. "I'd hoped to see you on the sidelines during our practice sessions."

"Josh gets embarrassed if I hang around too much."

"My mother did that all the time. I used to hate it, but deep down, I knew she couldn't help it. A hen protecting her chick."

"Are you her only son?"

His face turned grim. "Her only child, period. And she never lets me forget it. What about you?"

"My mother and father are still together, and I have one brother. They live in East Los Angeles. I grew up there."

He pursed his lips. "Oh? So you *are* like me. A stranger in a foreign land."

She laughed. "Moving from LA to Bay Point was definitely culture shock. But I like it here, and I hope you do, too."

"I'm liking it more and more."

Though his words seemed fraught with meaning, she was too afraid of disappointment to probe them further. *At least in person*, she thought, knowing she would analyze them later.

"Too bad you're only here for a while."

Her subtle yet hopeful hint, cloaked in a steady voice, was quickly shot down.

"Like I said before, when the high school soccer season ends, I'll be moving on."

She hitched her shoulders back. "Oh? Where to?"

He shrugged, but there was a look of assurance in his eyes. "Not sure. Maybe back home. Maybe somewhere else in the States."

She heard his words, loud and clear, though somehow they still managed to prick her heart. Her only recompense was that Sam's tone seemed less resolute, though it still had the edge of someone who could not stay in one place for too long.

A few nights ago she'd finally given in to the temptation and did a search on Sam on the internet. She knew from her son that he was a popular player, but she didn't know just how much.

It was shocking to learn he had suffered an injury to his left leg. It had sidelined him from soccer, though perhaps not permanently, as per the London gossip blogs. She'd also found plenty of articles about his playboy antics.

Mariella had little interest in being just another point on his scoreboard, but she was unashamed that on many sleepless nights, she toyed with the idea. Flirtation, she reasoned, as long as it was out of sight and hearing from her child, was harmless. No chance of a broken heart.

Sam snapped his fingers. "There's one thing I'm missing from Josh. The medical release forms. He never turned them in."

"Thank goodness I keep a copy of everything. I'll be right back."

She left the room and went into her office. It was in the back of her home, next to the kitchen, and looked out onto her garden. The forms were filed away in a two-pocket folder where she kept all important school paperwork.

Back in the living room, she found Sam standing near the fireplace. It had a stone front and mahogany mantel, and was one of her favorite places in the house. She set the document on the coffee table and went to join him there.

He picked up a picture of her and Josh in a silver frame. She was hugging him tightly, and he was smiling.

"You two look adorable. I can tell how much you love each other. How old was he?"

Her eyes smarted with sudden tears, and she turned away and pretended to cough so he wouldn't see.

It took only seconds to compose herself. "About five, and don't ask how old I was," she warned.

"I wouldn't dare." He put the photo back on the mantel. "We British have been known to be polite, reserved and very private. You never know what we are thinking."

She opened her mouth, wanting to ask him what he thought of her. Was she just another soccer mom to him or could she be something more?

"Fine, old construction. Reminds me of home," he said with a knock on the wood. "Does it ever get chilly enough in California to light this thing?"

"In the wintertime, the nights can get cool. You'll see."

"Maybe someday, if I get too cold and you get too cold, I can come over and light it for you. We could sit in front of the fire."

"And do what?" she blurted. "Talk about soccer?"

Without waiting for an answer, she hurried back to the coffee table. In the rush, she brushed against a stack of old magazines. They tumbled onto the table, sending Josh's medical forms to the floor.

"I should have stapled them together," she muttered.

"Let me help," Sam offered.

Mariella barely heard him she was so frustrated with herself as she knelt down. Chin to her chest, robe tucked between her legs, she set about picking up the mess.

He knelt down next to her. "You want to know what I would talk about?"

She looked up at him and shook her head.

"How beautiful you are."

Her hand paused at his words, heat wafting over her

face. It had been a while since she'd heard them from a man as handsome and accomplished as Sam. But could she believe him?

Since their brief time alone on the soccer field, her mind was in a haze. Thoughts of Sam crept up often throughout the day, and nights were preoccupied with fantasies that would likely never come true.

Sometimes she felt like her dating life was over, so his compliments were a great boost to her ego. But what good were they, if nothing could ever happen between them?

What did he stand to gain from giving her compliments, especially since he did not plan on staying in town? By the time spring rolled around, he would be on a plane, back to wherever.

She dropped her chin back to her chest, confused and barely able to look at him, and went back to picking up the papers.

"Is that what you think, or is that what you know?"

Sam stopped her hand and she lifted her face to his.

"It's what I see."

Mariella held her breath as he touched the middle of her bottom lip with his finger, let it trail down her chin, then along her jaw.

"It's what I wish I could feel, more than what I'm doing right now."

His caress didn't go any farther than the tip of her earlobe, yet she felt it all the way down to her loins.

Mariella didn't know where Josh was, but he could walk in the house at any time. It forced her from the tenderness of the moment back to reality.

She shied away from his touch and whispered, "You don't mean that. I know how you are."

"You do? How?"

Her eyes met his. "I know what I've read."

He dropped his hand into his lap. "Ah. My past has followed me, courtesy of the internet."

"Photos don't lie."

Sam waved her comment away with both hands. "Photos and stories can be doctored. Funny, you struck me as the type of woman who wouldn't read that trash."

She lifted her chin, even though his tone made her feel slightly ashamed. "I didn't want to read it."

"Then why did you?"

She handed him the forms, which he promptly rolled up and stuck under his arm. "I was curious about you."

He stood. "Ever hear of asking someone outright?"

Mariella refused his outstretched hand as she got to her feet, knowing that if she grabbed onto it, she might never let go.

"I couldn't. I don't even know you."

"Exactly."

He clipped out the word, and there was a sharper edge to his accent she didn't like. His whole demeanor changed. An invisible wall was put up that hadn't been there before, and Mariella knew that it was her fault.

Sam backed into the hallway. "Tell Josh if he misses another practice, without a medical excuse, he's off the team. No exceptions."

He was out the door before she could ask any questions. Mariella hurried to the living room curtains and as she watched him drive away, she realized she'd forgotten to tell him about the barbecue she hosted every year for the team on the night before their first game. Worse, she'd also likely destroyed her chances of ever getting to know the real Sam Kelly.

On his way home, Sam spotted Josh walking on the side of the road, backpack slung over his shoulders, about a

Winning Her Holiday Love

mile from downtown Bay Point. Head down, hands shoved in his front pockets.

Even from a distance, the boy appeared troubled.

Though he hardly knew Josh, concern arrowed its way through him, and as he got closer he honked his horn.

Josh didn't look up. Whether that was because of the headphones over his ears, or he recognized Sam's car, he didn't know.

Traffic was light, and when it was safe, he turned on the silver SUV's hazard lights, and made an awkward U-turn. He wasn't sure if he'd ever get used to the steering wheel being on the left side of the car, as opposed to the right as it was in the UK.

When he was on the other side of the road, he rolled down the passenger-side window and slowed the vehicle to a crawl.

"Hey, Josh! Get in!"

The boy looked over, eyes widening as recognition dawned.

"Coach? What are you doing here?"

"Looking for you. Hop in. I'll give you a ride home."

He shifted his backpack uneasily and kept walking as Sam rolled alongside, but stopped moments later.

Sam braked hard and looked into the rearview mirror at the same time. He breathed a sigh of relief to see there were no cars behind him. He reached over and pushed the door open.

"Geez, Coach. Watch it!"

He didn't look scared, just shocked.

"Sorry," Sam muttered as he looked into the rearview mirror. Several cars were slowing down behind him, so he rolled down his window and waved them on.

"Get in, will you? We're holding up traffic."

"I don't need a ride. I live just up the road."

Josh glanced both ways, as if contemplating his next course of action.

"I know where you live. Get in anyway."

Sam swallowed a groan when Josh hesitated again.

He'd only been coaching for a week, and he'd already learned how overly sensitive teenagers could be. Sometimes just changing his tone of voice made a world of difference in how they reacted to his instructions and guidance.

"I just want to talk to you," he said, hoping he sounded more reassuring.

Josh shrugged his shoulders, got in the car and slammed the door shut.

Sam exhaled a breath of relief and checked the rearview mirror once more. The road was clear of traffic, and he merged onto it.

"When you didn't show up today, I went to your house."

Josh slumped down in his seat. "My mom knows I wasn't at practice, too?"

Sam nodded, and turned off the hazard lights.

"Ah, man." He leaned his head back and groaned. "That also means she knows I lied to her."

"Right again, mate." He paused a beat. "So, do you want to tell me why you skipped out on your obligations today?"

Josh looked down at his hands and mumbled, "I don't know. I just didn't feel like going to practice."

He glanced over. "Take those headphones off, please. I have something important to say."

When they were in Josh's lap, Sam continued. "You want to be part of this team, you have to come to practice, no matter what. Is that clear?"

He wanted to cringe at the parental tone of his voice, and would rather be barking out ways to improve a kid's soccer skills than sternly admonishing bad teenage habits.

"My leg hurt today."

Josh's voice was low, and from the tone of it, Sam could tell the words probably hurt more.

"I told you if it got bad, you could sit on the bench."

"But I'm afraid if I do, you'll bench me for good!" Josh accused.

Sam knew from experience how difficult it was to admit pain, but he couldn't let Josh use that as an excuse.

"The only way that will happen is if you stop showing up, and you stop trying on the field."

He braked for a red light and turned his head. "You think I don't know what it's like to have an injury? To be afraid of the pain?"

"I'm *not* afraid," Josh interrupted.

The light turned over to green and Sam continued as if he hadn't heard.

"But that's no reason to stop playing the game you love. Your doctor felt you were physically ready. Now you just have to work on being mentally ready, too."

"I told you I'm not afraid." He gave an exasperated huff and turned away, brooding.

Sam figured he was either trying to take it all in, or dreaming up more excuses. Lately, with his own injury, he was adept at doing the latter.

"I'm sorry for being a loser today."

Sam shot Josh a hard glance, but he was still facing the window. "I don't coach losers. If aspects of your playing are different because of the injury, identify it and I can help you," he added. "As I stated, I've been there. I know what it's like."

"So if you're all recovered, why did you quit the pros?"

Sam pulled up to the curb beside Mariella's home. "I'm *mostly* recovered. I still do physical therapy, too," he clarified, nudging Josh's arm playfully. "And I didn't quit. I just took some time off to coach you rotten bunch of blokes."

"Thanks, Coach." Josh smiled shyly. "For the ride, and for the advice."

He draped his wrist over the steering wheel. "You're welcome. Now, what are you going to tell your mom?"

"The truth," Josh said without any hesitation.

"Great answer." Sam nodded. "See you tomorrow."

When Josh was safely inside, Sam drove downtown.

All the holiday decorations were up and the little town looked like it had been transported back to the time of Charles Dickens, without the snow. The streetlamps were wrapped with pine boughs and white lights. Each one of the "frosted" windows had a vintage holiday scene and he'd heard this was the first year all the stores were leased and open for business.

He was surprised to see so many people out and about on a weeknight. Couples arm in arm and families with kids browsing the shops, which were open late for holiday shopping. The old-fashioned carousel, smack dab in the middle of the square, was whirling slowly, lights twinkling merrily. With his window rolled down, he could hear the carnival-like strains of Christmas music and he smiled.

In general, he was pleased with his temporary home. Bay Point was charming and had more restaurants than he'd expected, though it could use a few more pubs. The people were friendly, sometimes overly so, but they seemed to mean him no harm. The beautiful beaches and temperate weather made him forget to be homesick for London and the career he'd left behind.

As he steered his SUV around the back of the building, he wondered if he would run into his landlord, Henry Wexler, the owner of Relics and Rarities. Short and squat, Wexler's rounded belly was always the first to show around a corner, and it swung like a pendulum whenever he moved.

He was shocked to learn his mother already knew the

man. They'd met at an antiques show in London, and had kept in touch over the years. She utilized Wexler's extensive contacts to add to her collection of English porcelain, and from what his mother told him, he was always glad to assist. It made him wonder if the apartment vacancy hadn't been prearranged.

Sam shook his head again, as he did after he'd ended that particular call with his mother. Just when he thought he knew everything about the woman who had borne him, he realized he didn't know anything at all. Except that she would love the tea set he'd sent to her.

He grabbed his duffel bag and climbed the stairs to his place. Compared to his tiny apartment in Bay Point, his flat on Farnborough Close, Brent, a borough of London, was a palace. Still, it suited him. Though he had plenty of money, he preferred to live in comfort, not over-the-top glitz.

He just hoped he wouldn't regret his decision to come over to the States and take this job in the first place.

His publicist told Sam that coaching in the United States was a great way to build his name on this side of the pond. Soccer was rapidly growing in popularity here, with professional teams sprouting up in several major cities. The sport, called football everywhere else except the US, had a worldwide appreciative fan base that bordered on mania.

His mother tried to guilt him out of it, by claiming he could heal up in London just as well as he could in California. He knew she would have been perfectly happy if he'd stayed in England, feeling sorry for himself.

Sam never claimed to be a self-aware kind of guy. He fully admitted to himself on a daily basis that he didn't know what he wanted, except to get away.

Brent, the town where he was born, was home to the legendary Wembley Stadium, the home of English football, and a place dear to his heart. He'd played on its famous pitch too many times to count. But his pride, his ego, not even the hordes of admiring females, could persuade him to stay.

He slung open the refrigerator and grabbed a light beer, cringing as he popped the cap off. The sound always brought him back to the day when his injury happened.

They were up a point and he'd been defending the team's hold on the ball. So intense was his focus, he didn't notice when another midfielder from the opposing team came after him at top speed and tried to steal it from him, until it was too late.

The crack of bone against bone.

The *pop* that filled his ears, and the instantaneous, gut-wrenching pain that faded his consciousness.

Emergency surgery was performed. Afterward, he awoke and learned he'd torn the anterior cruciate ligament, or ACL, on his left knee and bought himself an instant vacation. His career had come to a grinding halt and all his opponent got was a red penalty card. That they'd also won the game was the final, bruising blow.

Tears sprang to his eyes at the memory. He blamed it on sudden grogginess as vigorously as he pondered what would become of his fame.

All eyes had been watching Sam on the field that day. As soon as he hit the green pitch, knee twisted crazily to the side, the crowd began to root for him to get up.

To the average fan, soccer was something to watch and while away the hours of a day. To fantasize about being in the same cleats as a favorite pro player, dodging your opponent, trying to make the almighty goal, all the way to the bank.

But to him, soccer was his entire life and was for a long time. He'd been kicking that ball since he was six years old; had been playing professionally for ten. Now, at thirty-two, he may have to make other choices. Decisions he didn't even want to think about.

Sometimes life just wasn't fair.

"Go, Sammy! Get back in the game," he muttered to himself, but not even close to the vehemence of his so-called fans that day. Back in Brent, he'd never wondered if they really cared about him, or if they cared about the game more.

He took a slug of beer and voted the latter. He was entertainment, a fantasy figure, and nothing more.

Sam finished off the beer, rinsed the bottle out and threw it in the recycling bin. He'd dismissed an earlier call from his mother. Now, as he did his nightly regimen of crunches on the floor, he debated calling her back.

Though he loved his mother, she was a bit overbearing. His dad, who loved watching him play professional soccer, died ten years ago. He knew she was lonely since his passing, but that didn't give her the right to try to run his life from afar.

One reason he'd taken the coaching gig was to prove he could teach soccer to someone else. So far, he seemed to be doing okay, and was actually enjoying it. Expectations were high, from the kids to the athletic director to the parents, but he kept his attitude positive. What mattered most was that he was still involved in the game that he loved so much. This little side gig gave him an opportunity to explore a second career, if he decided not to return to professional soccer.

Or if his injury decided it for him.

Sam felt his phone vibrate in his pocket and he slid it on.

"You're up late. Did you get my gift?"

"Yes. I loved it."

"Excellent. Henry helped me pick it out. Otherwise, I probably would have chosen something tacky."

"Yes, Henry does have great taste. You, on the other hand, often do not. I was pleasantly surprised."

Sam grinned. "I can always count on you to be forthright, Mother. Anyway, what's up?"

"When are you coming back home?"

He knew, by the tone of her voice, that she had settled back into her favorite floral easy chair, and expected a prompt answer. The one *she* wanted to hear. Unfortunately, he couldn't give it to her.

"I'm not sure when or if I'll be back," he hedged. "I'm here until March at least."

She sighed heavily. "Are you at least coming home for Christmas? I want you to help me decorate."

During the holidays especially, his mother was more needy, and anxious to spend as much time with him as she could. The only reason she probably didn't follow him from country to country during the soccer season, which in Europe was most of the year, was because it would be too taxing for her.

Buying antiques was expensive therapy, but at least it kept her out of his hair.

"Probably not, Mum. I'll probably stay in Bay Point for Christmas," he replied, refusing to confirm his whereabouts so far in advance. "At least the paparazzi aren't following my every move here."

"That's all part of being a star," his mother urged.

"Sometimes I think you like it more than I do," he grumbled.

"What mother in the free world doesn't want her child to be popular?" she harped with a disgusted snort.

He rolled up into a sitting position. "I don't know. Fame sometimes feels fake to me."

"Why should it? You've earned every flash, every bit of ink, real and virtual."

"I never wanted it," he insisted, steadying his elbow on his good knee.

"That's what makes it so perfect," she reasoned, and then paused for a long moment. "Haven't I given you everything you've ever wanted?"

He heard her sniffling back tears. Though he didn't know if they were genuine or for show, his voice softened.

"Yes, of course you have, Mum."

"Then why not give me something I want. Come back home to Brent where you belong. You can go back to playing soccer. Or you can just relax until you figure out what you want to do."

"I don't know. I'm not ready to decide yet."

"Are they even paying you?"

He rolled his eyes at the question.

"We worked out an arrangement."

"How much?" she demanded.

He held the phone away from his ear, thumb poised over the end call button.

"Don't make me be rude, Mother."

His mother had provided everything necessary for a child to survive: food, clothing, shelter. His father, an investment banker, worked a lot of hours to afford the expensive roof over their heads, and the jewels on his wife's fingers. She'd loved him and been his rock when his father was too busy with his business affairs.

He hated when she treated him as if he was still a teenager, and recalled when he'd made the mistake of telling her how much he was earning as a bagger at the local grocery store. She'd gone up to the shopkeeper and demanded he give her son a raise, and the man ended up firing him.

She huffed out a breath in a way that made him even angrier. "It can't be nearly as much as you could make playing pro soccer."

Sam got up and paced the living room. He knew he'd reached a point in the conversation that would make it a struggle to keep his voice calm.

"Of course it's not, but I don't need any more money. What I need is—"

Mariella.

Her name popped into his head, when normally he would have told his mother he needed to be left alone.

Before she could argue with him further, he told her he was tired and hung up.

Afterward, Sam cleaned his apartment. He was the only man he knew who cleaned for relaxation. It didn't hold a candle to great sex, but that wasn't an option right now.

For most of his dating years, he'd been with women who had not been worth the effort or the risk to be a better man.

Too often, he would drown his sorrows in the arms of a woman he didn't really want, at least for more than a night. A woman he knew he would never, and couldn't ever, love for a lifetime.

When he was in his early twenties, he'd started to care deeply for a woman. It ended the day she sold the story about their relationship to the London gossip magazines. Her betrayal hurt him to the core, and now he was very wary of trusting any woman, especially when there was an instant attraction.

He didn't know when he realized he needed the love of a woman who could see past his so-called fame, into the person he was inside. Maybe it was when he was laid up in a hospital bed for a month, when the steady stream of visitors dried up, and so did his coverage in the newspapers. He'd had plenty of time to think, to review what had occurred in his life up until then, and he learned he was still very much a secret to himself.

For so long, he'd been focused on life "outward"—

success, money and prestige. There was still so much about him he needed to discover, and he didn't want to go at it alone.

He retreated to his bedroom and separated his dirty clothes into piles by color. His apartment did not have a washer and dryer. There was a laundromat close by that had pick-up and drop-off service; all he had to do was place the call. He dreaded doing his own laundry, so he appreciated the amenity.

Around eleven, he hopped into the shower. Despite the fact that he'd been out of Mariella's presence for several hours, he couldn't shake the longing he felt for her. It was as if she were right in front of him, and he grabbed his penis, imagining her watching him as he stroked and stroked.

He saw her naked before him, the hot water coursing between her breasts and sliding down both of their bodies. Her eyes trained on his fist moving faster and faster as he watched her hands stroke between her spread legs.

It wasn't long until he was limp, energy spent, panting with his forehead against tile. Mariella evaporated in his mind as the water ran cool down his back, ending his fantasy.

Later in bed the sheets were cold, scratchy and unwelcoming. Sam thought how nice it would be to have Mariella beside him, wrapped in his arms. Then he counted the months he had remaining in Bay Point.

With a sad sigh, he decided his fantasies were safer for both of them, plumped his pillow and fell asleep.

Chapter 4

Sam blew his whistle hard. He threw his hands up high into the air as if it could rid him of the intense frustration he was feeling.

"C'mon, guys! What's the matter with you?" His players stopped in their tracks. None of them was where he'd instructed them to be on the field.

"Huddle up," he shouted.

When they all assembled in front of him, he dropped his whistle against his team polo shirt and gave them his sternest look.

"Have you guys forgotten? Tomorrow is our first game!"

The Titans were playing against the Bulldogs. In the past, the Bulldogs had been one of the worst teams in the district. Sam knew better than to trust they would fare the same this season. Underdog teams had nowhere to go but up.

Dante scoffed, and puffed out his chest. "We beat them last year, and the year before, with our hands tied behind our backs."

Sam crossed his arms against Dante's know-it-all attitude. Even though he was one of his best players, he wasn't going to allow Dante to circumvent his authority.

"Don't count the Bulldogs out yet. I went and watched a scrimmage match a couple of days ago, and they've got a couple of new juniors who are blazing down the field." He waved his clipboard in the air. "A lot more than I can say for most of you today."

Some of the boys grumbled aloud in response. Others stabbed at the dirt with the toes of their cleats, actions that also rankled his nerves. Most, however, appeared to be listening to him.

Sam stuck his clipboard under his arm and slammed his fist down onto his open palm. His words may have been harsh, but he wasn't about to sugarcoat the facts.

"Winning doesn't happen with a click of a button. It requires constant diligent improvement on the part of each member of this team so we can all perform at the highest level at all times."

He wiped the sweat from his palms on his black shorts. "Let's try that formation again," he barked, clapping his hands together to get their attention. "And put some life in it."

Josh stepped forward out of the pack, uniform shirt sticking to his chest. "We can do it, Coach." He glanced back at his teammates. "Right, guys?"

All of them were nodding, except for Dante.

Sam raised an eyebrow, pleased it was Josh who was encouraging the rest of the team. Maybe it was because he wanted to be selected as team captain, an honor bestowed on a deserving senior who showed the most leadership potential.

"I'm counting on it," Sam said with deliberate gruffness. "Watch those ruts!"

He warned them daily to be careful, but also didn't want

the condition of the field to drastically affect the way each one of them played.

The boys ran off, and when they were in place, he blew his whistle. This time around, they had more energy, and Josh even scored the winning goal for his scrimmage team.

Sam, pacing the sidelines, instructed them to drill the formation a few more times, until practice was over.

"Great job, Josh!" Mariella yelled out.

He whirled around, being careful of his bad knee, and saw her standing a few feet behind him. She was struggling to hold on to two bulging grocery bags.

"Let me help you with those," he called out.

The cautious smile he got back was worth the interruption.

Without waiting for an answer, he took the bags from her and set both on a nearby bench.

"Thanks." She whooshed out a breath. "Those were heavy."

"What are you doing here?"

He hoped he didn't sound like he didn't want her around. Quite the opposite. He'd missed her.

It was the first time seeing her since he'd stormed out of her home. He'd wanted to call her and tell her he was sorry, but he also knew it was always better to apologize in person.

"Tim's mother called and said she couldn't bring the snacks today."

He frowned as he watched her shake what he assumed was a cramp out of her hands.

"I hope it isn't anything serious."

"She told me she had to go pick up her youngest from school. Not sure of the reason, and it's really none of my business. I was next on the list, so here I am."

"I'm glad to see you. I'm sorry about our conversation. It ended badly."

Her eyes gleamed with surprise, and she glanced around briefly.

"Did you miss me?" Her voice was almost a whisper.

Sam didn't want to ask if she'd been avoiding him, but if she thought staying away from him could make him want her any less, she was wrong. He fought the urge to touch her cheek, and instead held the clipboard at his waist.

"I haven't seen you anywhere but in my mind in over a week."

He wanted to tell her he wished she were in that white robe she'd worn, teasing him with her slim, brown, bare legs.

Without moving his head, he took his time reviewing her long-sleeve, light yellow button-down shirt and a navy skirt with a sweater tied around her shoulders. Today her attire was all business, and she wore it to perfection.

"Then I accept your apology." She smiled, and seemed not to notice his open perusal of her. His dark sunglasses worked their magic once again.

"I work full-time, so I can't attend too many practices, but most parents don't, right?"

He nodded. "Dante's mother is here for almost all of them, but I gather that's because she doesn't have anything else to do."

"Except gossip," Mariella giggled.

Sam wasn't even going to touch that one. He pointed to her fuchsia-and-blue footwear. "Love the sneakers."

"Thanks. I changed out of my pumps in the car. My heels would have sunk in this dirt."

"You're very wise. I would mention you look very pretty today, but I don't want to be accused of flirting."

"I won't tell if you won't," she teased and then turned to dig into the grocery bags.

The straightness of her back flowed into a bottom so

round it made him go stiff. With a low groan, he planted the clipboard in front of his waist again.

"Hmm...could be dangerous, pretty lady."

She turned, glanced at him over her shoulder and smiled, seeming not to notice his predicament. He waited a minute until it was safe to put the clipboard down on the bench. Then he helped her set out prepackaged cheese and crackers, a variety of yogurts and fruit. Another parent had already dropped off a cooler stocked with Gatorade and waters.

When they were done, Sam stepped back a few paces to appraise their work, and Mariella.

"The guys will appreciate these snacks. They've been pretty sluggish all afternoon, until your son stepped up and gave them a pep talk."

"Really? Josh did? I'm surprised. He's usually not that encouraging to himself, let alone others. You must be a good influence on him."

She folded her arms over her chest, and he batted away thoughts of his hands there instead.

"Now who's flirting with whom?" His heart dug a new well of hope when she returned his sardonic smile.

Sam turned his back to the field, creating what he hoped was a wall of temporary privacy for the two of them.

"I really am sorry the way our conversation ended the last time we were together."

She put her hands on her hips and took a step toward him, almost close enough for him to feel the heat from her body.

"I will only forgive you if you promise to behave yourself going forward."

He leaned in close enough to smell the sweet rose-scented spice of her perfume. "That's a promise I'm not sure I can keep."

Her mouth parted and before Sam could give in to the strong urge to kiss her, he turned away. His whole body ached with need, and the sooner he got away from Mariella, the sooner he could get back to focusing on what was most important.

Preparing for the team's first game.

He lifted his whistle to his lips, and felt Mariella's hand on his arm. He turned and searched her eyes.

"What is it? Practice is nearly over, and I have to give the guys some final feedback."

"This won't take long. I have good news. I spoke to the principal a couple of days ago, and received an email from him today."

She clasped her hands together, and her eyes lit up with excitement. "He wants to set up a meeting with you, me, Leslie, and Brian Putnam, your boss, to discuss."

"Why Leslie?" he asked, still holding on to the whistle.

"She's the president of the PTA. Remember?"

He let the whistle slack against his chest. "Oh, yeah. No wonder she's been hanging around, spying on me."

Mariella shook her head. "I don't think so. She probably thinks you're cute."

He shrugged, knowing he couldn't care less what Leslie thought about him. He only cared about Mariella, although a lot of good it was doing him.

"Anyway, that *is* great news. Thanks for helping to kickstart this project. I'll help in any way I can."

"No problem," Mariella said. "We can talk about it more tonight."

Sam scratched his head in confusion. "Tonight?"

"The potluck barbecue at my house," Mariella replied. "Didn't Josh tell you?"

He rocked back and forth on his heels, not quite believing his good fortune. Since it would have been inappropriate to ask her out on a date, he'd been hoping for an opportunity to spend some time with her. Now he would just have to find a way to talk to her alone.

"I heard some discussion about it, but I didn't know I was invited."

"Of course you are. I have it for the team every year. In fact, you're the guest of honor."

"Then I wouldn't miss it for the world."

Mariella smoothed her dress and took one last look in the mirror. On impulse, she swirled around once more, admiring the garment's deep purple hue. It was one of her favorite colors to wear in autumn and winter.

Her excitement grew as her fingers traced the white piping along the scoop neckline, which also trimmed the bell-capped sleeves and hem, and played nicely with her nut-brown skin.

Although she could have worn jeans and a T-shirt, as host of the event, she always dressed up.

Her mother taught her to look beautiful for herself first, instead of for a man. She'd never understood that concept until she moved to Bay Point, where she knew no one, and was so focused on parenting her child she'd relinquished dating.

"Men come and go," her mother used to say as she braided Mariella's long black hair, "but we women must go on."

Unfortunately, her mother, who believed in "mind over matter," never agreed with her decision to move, while her dad knew that sometimes a change in environment was best, and helped pay for her moving expenses.

There were so many times Mariella thought her mother was right. That she had made a mistake in moving to Bay Point. But for Josh's sake, she'd made the best of the situation. Landing the job at the mayor's office, getting her degree, making new friends. Now it was time to put a renewed focus on her.

She dabbed some of her favorite perfume behind her ears, and didn't feel at all guilty for wanting and needing to look good tonight.

For herself, but also for Sam.

When he'd visited her home, she'd outwardly rejected his flirting, though inwardly she'd loved the attention. Seeing him again that afternoon made her realize that perhaps she'd been too hasty. She was tired of putting aside her needs, her desires, but she still had to be discreet.

Mariella brushed her hair out in long strokes, and sighed at her reflection in the mirror. She almost wished she were a teenager again, doodling hearts in notebooks, unconcerned about what people would say, or think, or do.

Whether he deserved it or not, Sam had a reputation as a playboy, and in some respects that was immensely freeing.

She didn't have to worry about him committing to her, because his track record indicated he wouldn't. So she was off the hook, too. She just needed to decide in her mind that she could handle having a little fun, without the labels, the love or the commitment.

Mariella shut the door to her bedroom and went downstairs. Her guests would be arriving soon and she wanted to double-check that everything was ready.

She'd hosted the barbecue for both the boys' and girls' junior varsity and varsity soccer teams for the past three years, offering up her home and her yard, both of which were quite large, for a few hours. It helped ingratiate her and Josh into the Bay Point community, particularly the soccer moms.

It was also her belief that the event helped her win her bid to be vice president of the PTA, a role she really enjoyed. Being involved in the organization kept her close to key staff at the school, apprised of many upcoming changes and allowed her to feel she had a purpose in Josh's education, besides being a worrywart.

The gathering was potluck, so that kept her costs down. She supplied the beverages, plates, utensils and paper products. The soccer team always cleaned up, as best a group of teenagers could, she mused to herself.

Some parents stayed for the event, but some did not. Most of the single parents chose to drop off their dishes and pick their kids up later. She was never offended, and could certainly empathize with the need to have some alone time.

Mariella ventured outside. Her backyard was extensive, and bordered by native California perennial wildflowers. The grass was green and lush, watered by an underground irrigation system.

"How does it look?" Josh asked.

He'd covered the ten folding tables she'd borrowed from the school with gold vinyl tablecloths. There were sprigs of fresh purple and red mums in small bud vases on every one, and the potluck table had all the plates and utensils neatly placed on one end.

She appraised her son's long shorts and T-shirt emblazoned with the logo of one of his favorite basketball teams. He'd recently started taking greater care of his appearance, and she was proud of him for it.

"Everything looks great, and so do you," she replied and gave him an awkward sideways hug. "The last thing I need you to do is to check that we have a nice mixture of beverages in the coolers."

"Sure, Mom."

He lumbered off, his limp barely visible now.

To her relief, he'd even started doing his physical therapy exercises on a regular basis, and without being asked.

She didn't know what was the motivating factor in Josh's life, but she was sure Sam had something to do with it. He'd had a positive influence on her, why not her son?

Since Josh's father had died, Mariella always felt he needed a strong male role model. Her own father had tried, but when they moved to Bay Point, he and her mom only visited about six times in three years.

A slight breeze lifted the ends of her hair as she picked up and moved the folding chairs into small clusters to encourage conversation. The weather was unseasonably warm for November. She straightened a stack of light-weight, cotton throw blankets, which she'd placed in a large wicker basket. They were there for the taking in case any of her guests got chilly as the night wore on.

Mariella glanced over at the hedges surrounding the house. They were strung with multicolored Christmas lights, providing a festive glow. She'd thought of every-thing, down to the sign on the front door directing guests to the backyard, except how hard it would be to hide her attraction to Sam.

In the spirit of the season, she'd simply have to be nice, not naughty, she thought with a decided jerk of her chin.

The first to arrive to the potluck was Emily Stego and her mother.

Emily played goalie on the varsity girls' team, and was also Josh's first crush. She was probably the reason why he was paying so much attention to his clothes and hair. Mariella sincerely hoped Josh would work up the courage to ask Emily out on a date.

"One last soiree," Emily's mother commented.

Mariella led the way to the potluck table. She'd forgot-ten the woman's name, and was too embarrassed to ask.

"Yes, since this is Josh's senior year, someone else will have to take over hosting these next year."

Emily's mom set down a macaroni casserole. "Your house is perfect for the occasion."

"Thank you, but I'm sure a suitable replacement can be found," she replied, smiling.

"The beverages are in the coolers over there under the trees, if you'd care for a soda or water."

More guests arrived, including the assistant coaches and their families. Mariella excused herself to go and greet them.

In a short time, the main entrée table was laden with a variety of foods, including some very appetizing vegetarian options.

She was organizing the desserts on a separate table when she heard a chorus of shouts, and then a rousing, though off-key, rendition of the Bay Point High School anthem.

She turned, and as Sam rounded the corner of her house, the boys and girls in the backyard erupted into applause. The parents and coaches quickly joined in and so did she.

"It's the man of the hour!" she called out.

There were a few "hear, hears" from the adults in the crowd, and Sam bowed in response.

Mariella couldn't help but notice how handsome he looked in tailored blue pants and a white polo shirt that stretched along his chest and biceps.

Leslie accompanied him, her arm looped through his. Her husband was nowhere in sight. She felt a pang of jealousy, and was disgusted by it, but there it was.

She reached for the square glass pan of brownies he held in his hands, and smiled. "Hello, Mr. Guest of Honor. You didn't have to bake."

Leslie beat her to it, and claimed the brownie pan.

"He didn't bake these. They're mine. All Sam needs to do is win games."

Sam stepped out of the realm of both women and motioned for his team to gather around him.

"And we will, right, team?"

With hoots and hollers, the boys agreed. The girls and their coaches joined in the mini pep rally, too.

Throughout the evening, everyone clamored around Sam. She noticed he barely had an opportunity to eat, so she fixed him a plate, wedged through the crowd and brought it over to him.

"We can't win if our coach starves to death."

He took the plate from her and her heart raced at the huge smile on his face. She knew it was meant just for her.

"I'm fine, Ms. Vency. Thank you."

She left and floated from group to group, making sure her guests had what they needed, all the while trying to keep her eyes from tracking Sam.

Emily's mom was gone and Josh was at Emily's side. It was sweet to see them talking, their heads bent toward each other, and she wished she could talk to Sam in the same manner. As the festivities wound to a close, she put out some plastic containers so people could take home leftovers, and then headed back inside to the kitchen.

She filled one side of her sink with clean, soapy water. Not wanting her guests to take a dirty dish back home, she always offered to wash their empty casserole pans.

Sam peeked his head in the door. "Need some help?"

She nodded, more out of shock he was there than actually needing his assistance.

"I'll take that as a yes."

His eyes widened at the stack of casserole dishes, and he grabbed a sponge from the front edge of the double-bowled sink.

"Plus, I owe you for feeding me."

She looked at him askance, and when she inhaled the scent of his musky cologne, knew that if she got any closer it would be very tough not to be naughty.

"Are you sure you're up to this? You're a popular guy. You have to keep your strength up to sign all those autographs."

"I'd rather be here, with you, scraping grease off pans."

Mariella grinned and waved a soapy hand in front of her face, in tandem with her heart fluttering in her chest.

"How romantic."

Both of her hands were submerged, and she watched in fascination as his left hand sank into the clean water. It tangled with hers, massaging her knuckles gently.

"I haven't even gotten started."

She hitched in a breath and stared outside, and saw members of the soccer team cleaning up. It only made Sam's movements and the sensations she was experiencing as he stroked her fingers under the water more intimate.

Mariella turned to look at him, her heart beating even more wildly now. "Sam, don't."

She jerked her chin toward the window. "Someone could come in and see."

He removed his hands slowly, and then flicked some suds toward her. "You're no fun."

"I am, too," she protested, despite his good-natured tone. "Under the right conditions."

"And doing dishes together isn't one of them?"

She laughed. "Usually not."

"I bet I can persuade you." He leaned his right hip against the sink, stuck his hand inside the water and began to massage her hands again.

"I'm only doing this because the water is clean."

She laughed, stared into his eyes and quickly looked away in case anyone outside glanced over at the window.

"I'm glad you have some standards."

"I do. And you beat them all."

Her face heated, and he started to work his way to her wrist, and then up her arm.

Suddenly, she heard the sound of the kitchen door opening. It was Leslie, a disconcerting smirk on her face.

Had she seen?

Sam jerked his hands out of the sink and grabbed a nearby dishtowel. She grabbed a casserole dish and plunged it deep into the water. When little bits of brownie floated to the surface, she realized the dish belonged to Leslie.

Leslie looked at the two of them, and Mariella could practically see the wheels of the gossip machine that lived in her brain turning.

"Hey, some of the parents are looking for you," she said, addressing Sam. "They want to say goodbye."

"Go on, Sam," Mariella urged. "I can get these."

When Sam was gone, Leslie stepped into Sam's place, but did not offer to help.

"He's a nice guy, isn't he?" she asked.

Mariella shrugged. "Of course. Anyone can see that."

"You, more than anyone."

The bright pink headband she wore in her blond hair suddenly annoyed Mariella, almost as much as her line of questioning.

"What do you mean by that, Leslie?"

"He's single. You're single."

She turned on the faucet and rinsed the dish clean.

"So are a lot of people in Bay Point. What are you getting at?"

"Just be careful, Mariella. People see, and people talk. You don't want Sam to lose his coaching position because of inappropriate behavior, do you?"

She dried Leslie's baking dish and handed it to her.

"Don't worry about me, Leslie. I can take care of myself."

Chapter 5

Thirty minutes later the soccer players who remained helped load the folding tables into her car to be returned to the school on Monday, before leaving with their parents.

Josh decided to walk Emily home, and she and Sam waved goodbye to them from the top of the driveway.

Mariella went to the backyard, and smiled when he followed her. She grabbed a blanket from the basket and wrapped it around her shoulders. It was more a gesture of habit, rather than actually being cold.

Even though they hadn't done anything wrong, after the unsettling conversation with Leslie, her nerves were still on edge.

Mariella shivered, her body still humming with pleasure from Sam's touch. There was no reason for him to stay with her any longer, yet she was glad he didn't leave.

"Thanks for a great event."

"We had great weather, and I think everyone enjoyed themselves. That's all I can ask for."

"I stayed behind because I wanted to talk to you about Josh."

She hugged the blanket around her and frowned.

"What's the problem now? I thought you said today his playing had improved."

"It has, so much so that he is among those I'm considering for team captain."

She clapped her hands together, relieved. "He will be so excited if he's chosen."

Sam nodded. "I'm really happy with not only his performance, but also his leadership."

"Just don't push him too much. That's my job."

Her voice grew soft with regret. "Sometimes I feel like I expect too much from him. I'm being too overprotective, aren't I?"

He closed the gap between them and huddled the blanket more neatly around her shoulders.

"You're just being a mom. I wouldn't expect any less."

It wasn't the most romantic thing to say, but when Sam's forehead grazed hers, and idled there, she knew he wanted to kiss her. It was a tense crackle of an invite, tempting her to place her hands around his neck and make the first move.

She knew she should push him away, but she couldn't.

Leslie's warning, which in retrospect felt more like a subtle threat, waved a white flag in the back of her mind.

To quibble about its meaning would be to take herself out of the moment, but making the wrong choice could have lasting impact.

Then why did the wrong thing feel so right?

Face-to-face now, his gray eyes were ruminative and his brow furrowed as if he was thinking of the potential consequences, too. She couldn't read his mind, but she could feel the heat between them, threatening to ignite.

This was what she'd hoped for. A gorgeous man, his lips mere inches away, her body craving more.

She let the blanket fall to the ground.

There was a tangible sense that she should let go of herself and fall into him, but still she hesitated. Frozen in place, but melting underneath.

She brought her hand up to his face, likely smooth in the morning, rough stubble now in the night. His intake of breath was slight, like the breeze before a windstorm. In the moonlight, his eyes, blunt under the influence of desire, searched hers.

Closing her eyes, she felt his warm breath on her skin. His lips brushed hers, drawing in a searing pleasure in the pit of her stomach, and her toes to their tips.

Sam grasped her arms at her sides, and she stood frozen in place, kissing him back. Her desiring him, him wanting her, was like trying to wade out of quicksand. It was futile. Slowly, they would get sucked in and plunge into its depths.

But at least they'd have fun on the way down.

Suddenly, his phone buzzed against her upper thigh.

"Damn," he muttered. "I have to go."

"It's okay, Sam. I understand."

She thought it was odd he didn't check his phone to see who it was. Whoever it was, he or she was more important than being with her.

Sam reached for her hand and tried to bring it up to his lips, but she slipped away. The chaste kiss on the cheek he gave her before he left only heightened the sense that something had been lost, that she'd been cheated out of much-needed intimacy.

Back in the kitchen Mariella finished cleaning the rest of the dishes while waiting for Josh to return home.

The interruption was an unwanted wake-up call. A time

to step off, step back and face facts. She was treading on some very dangerous ground, and she wasn't the only one who could get hurt.

Sam turned off his phone, something he now wished he'd done prior to the party. He pulled out of Mariella's driveway, hating to leave her. Ever since they met, he'd known it would be a challenge to keep his attraction under wraps.

Tonight was no different.

God, he'd wanted to smash his lips on hers, make her a part of him and kiss her like she'd never been kissed before. He'd been so turned on, touching and massaging her hands in the soapy water, he'd nearly gone out of his mind.

At a red light, he closed his eyes briefly and saw again the disappointment on Mariella's face before he walked away.

She'd *wanted* him to kiss her, and keep on kissing her, perhaps for the rest of the night. They had shared a short but passionate kiss that was pleasurable for them both. Still, he didn't want to hurt her, and by the look in her eyes tonight, that was exactly what he did. She probably would never let him near her again.

Sam eased off the brake and continued on his way home, not at all eager to get to his quiet, lonely apartment.

Having traveled all over the world, Sam never wanted to settle down in one place or with one woman. He'd come to realize Mariella could change his mind, and that scared him. If anyone could move past his wealth, his fame and see he was really just a simple guy at heart, it would be her.

He wanted her, and for more than one night. The interruptions, first by Leslie, then by technology, should have deterred his lust, but they didn't.

Her beauty and sensual curves were a wonderful bonus.

Every time he saw her he was reminded of how tempting she was, but those weren't the main things that attracted him to her.

Mariella was down-to-earth, and he had a hunch she would be loyal to him, unlike some of the other women he'd allowed himself to be close to.

He licked his lips, but the taste of her was gone and he wasn't sure when he'd get the chance to kiss her again. The team's first game was tomorrow and he'd be incredibly busy for the next several weeks.

If she wants to see me, I'll make the time.

Sam rolled down his window and smiled warily. It felt good to make some sort of decision about their relationship, even if they were in the very early stages.

Breathing in the salt-scented air, he bypassed his apartment and decided to go to the beach for a while before going home. The sound of the waves would calm him down, so maybe he could get a good night's sleep.

He rubbed his stomach, remembering how Mariella had brought him a plate of food. The barbecue was more fun than he'd thought. The parents were friendly and welcoming, and he'd enjoyed sharing stories about his career as a pro player. Nobody asked for his autograph, or pressed him about when he'd be back playing full-time. For a few hours it was easy to forget he'd once been in the public eye.

It was a nice feeling. Being a normal guy, instead of a famous one. He'd grown tired of always being on guard. One wrong word, one date with the wrong woman, and heaven forbid, a mistake on the field, brought on a firestorm of media attention. In some cases, the stuff said about him was so outrageously untrue, he could have sued for libel.

In the last two months of his pro career, he had been so frustrated he just wanted the season to end.

"Be careful what you wish for," he muttered as he pulled into the beach parking lot.

Though he knew it was impossible, sometimes he wondered if he'd brought his injury upon himself. Maybe he'd wanted change so much, forces in the universe had worked to bring his life to a complete halt. Or perhaps he'd just had a run of bad luck.

Whatever the cause, it had led him to Bay Point, and Mariella. Meeting her was making him rethink his whole outlook on everything.

Sam selected a spot away from other vehicles and turned off the ignition. Though it was dark outside, it would be easy enough to walk down to the beach, kick off his shoes and dig his toes into the sand. But he decided to stay in his car. He powered on his phone and it rang almost immediately.

"Tell my mother the answer is no."

Niles, his sports agent, laughed. "Is that why you didn't pick up before? You know I can't do that. Nobody can."

Sam blew out a breath as his frustration came galloping back. "I have. Hundreds of times."

"And has she listened?"

"Never."

Niles chuckled again, and Sam wondered where he was this time. The short-statured man with a pudgy stomach and salt-and-pepper comb-over loved to travel to expensive locales where he could don his beloved Madras shorts, have a fruity cocktail and make deals for his clients.

"It's not just her, it's everyone in the country. Haven't you been reading the papers?"

Sam stared out his window at the waves, wishing he could dive in and disappear.

"Thankfully, I haven't seen those papers in the States. And I hate reading papers online."

"So do I, so I'll keep it brief," Niles replied begrudgingly. "I'm getting emails from fans around the world. I need you back on the field."

"No, you need an assistant." Sam smirked.

"Quite so." Niles laughed. "But he or she would never make me the kind of money I stand to make with you."

Sam could imagine Niles chewing on the end of one of the Cuban cigars he preferred, but never smoked.

"And nobody could stand being with you."

When Niles began to protest, Sam cut in. "Your words, not mine. Remember?"

"I just prefer to work alone. That's not wrong."

"Nor is me being tired of hearing how disappointed everyone is that I'm not playing for Valor anymore."

"You owe it to your fans!" Niles insisted.

Sam pinched the bridge of his nose to stem off the headache beginning to surface.

Just because he was famous didn't mean he was required to explain every decision. It wasn't the constant travel or the soccer groupies that seemed to follow him everywhere. He simply wanted a break. Time just for him, for reflection and for figuring out what he really wanted out of life.

"I don't owe anybody anything."

"You're sounding a bit like Scrooge, my friend."

"Bah humbug," Sam grumped in agreement.

"Listen to me, Sam. I'm concerned about your welfare. Guys as competitive and as talented as you are don't have an easy time transitioning out of the pros."

"I kind of had a little help, Niles. Care of three little letters. A-C-L. Remember?"

"You've got that beat. Are you seeing the physical therapist I told you about? And did you ever find a gym in that godforsaken town? It's important that you stay in shape."

Sam couldn't help but smile. Niles was obsessed with making money, but at least he made his clients feel cared about as he filled his own coffers.

"The therapist is great, I joined the gym the other day and by the way, I kind of like Bay Point."

Mariella had a lot to do with it, but that was none of his agent's business.

"I'm going to pretend I didn't hear you say that." Niles sounded aghast. "How is the coaching job?"

"It's fine. It's different than playing, for sure, but I like being able to run things my way."

"Taking some cues from your former coach?"

Leo Minor, apparently named for the lesser lion constellation, was prone to yelling and screaming to get his way. No guy wanted to be a victim of his very loud roar.

Sam grunted. "If I did, most of my team would probably quit."

"Regardless of his methods, he knew how to win."

"Be a good agent and wish me good luck. We have our first game tomorrow."

"I'm raising my cocktail in your honor," Niles replied. "I hope you're successful, but not too successful. I'm expecting you back in Brent in a few months."

"I'm not promising anything, Niles."

"Just promise me you'll look at some of the offers I emailed your way this morning," he begged.

"It's Saturday already for you. Go back to sleep."

Sam ended the call and tossed the phone onto the passenger seat, not caring if Niles was offended by his abruptness. But he felt even guiltier about leaving Mariella for a conversation that had only made him angry, and for putting soccer first, when in that passionate moment, that hadn't been necessary.

When he'd been recovering in the hospital, he'd begun

to realize how much of his life he'd lived on autopilot. Since childhood, he had been programmed to compete and to win, at all costs.

Now, unable to play at the same level he had before, his belief in himself had been crushed. He had to find something else, or someone else, to believe in.

Soccer just wasn't enough anymore.

He started the SUV and backed out of the empty lot.

Maybe it wasn't fair to either of them, and maybe it wasn't right, but he had to see Mariella again.

Tonight.

Leftovers are evil, Mariella thought as she made space for one more plastic container in the refrigerator. Most of her guests ignored her plea to take them home, probably figuring Josh would eat them.

They were right.

As soon as he returned from Emily's house, he had a snack before going upstairs. If he didn't consume the rest of the food by the end of the day tomorrow, into the trash it would go.

After washing her hands, she set the teakettle on the stove and turned on the gas. Then she unwrapped a piece of cake she'd managed to snag before it was all gone and placed it on the kitchen table. Since she was denied the sweetness of a longer kiss from Sam, she was going to enjoy every bite.

A gentle breeze rustled the yellow café curtains that hung at the window above the sink. She stood nearby and wondered if she'd ever wash another dish without thinking about Sam, or get an answer to the question that was on a constant loop in her mind.

Who had called him and what was so important he had to leave right away?

An insistent knock on the back door startled her. The teakettle whistled annoyingly at the same time. On tiptoe and on edge, she leaned over the sink, parted the curtains and looked out.

Sam! What was he doing back here?

Mariella rushed to the stove, turned off the kettle, and then walked calmly to the door and opened it.

He stood just outside the illuminating radius of the porch light, so his expression was unreadable. Though Mariella was excited to see him, she could only manage a tight smile.

"I didn't expect to see you until tomorrow, at the game."

"Can I come in?" he asked, with his hands behind his back. "I promise this won't take long."

She nodded and stepped back so Sam could close the door. When they got into the kitchen, he appeared troubled.

"I have a confession to make."

At his words, she put her hand on her chest, expecting the worst.

"What is it?"

He kept his eyes on hers, and his gaze was so penetrating and kind, she relaxed even though she didn't know what he was going to say.

"I missed you, and this time I couldn't go to sleep without letting you know it."

"You mean you've missed me before?"

Her innocent tone belied the torrent of warmth rushing through her veins. When he nodded, she dropped her hand to her hip and fought back a wide smile.

"You could have called."

He took a step toward her, reached out a hand and stroked her hair. "No, I had to say it in person. And more important, I wanted to apologize for leaving so suddenly."

Mariella resisted the urge to lean into his touch, not sure what he wanted from her.

"Is everything okay? Do you want to talk about it?"

"I do, but I'm not sure you will like what I have to say."

Her heart fell, and she backed away from him, glad she'd decided to be cautious.

"Why don't you let me be the judge? Would you care for some tea? The kettle is already hot."

He nodded and she walked over to the small cupboard that held all her teas. Her hand shook as she put one Orange Blossom tea bag each in two mugs, poured the water and brought them to the table. Sam declined her offer of sugar, honey or milk.

"I like my tea plain, too."

Mariella sat down next to him and dipped her tea bag back and forth in the water, before setting it on the saucer she'd placed on the table earlier.

Sam did the same, and when he was done, he took a tentative sip. "Delicious. Did you know in Great Britain, there's a science to making tea?"

Mariella gave him a wry glance. "It's just hot water and a tea bag. What's so scientific about it?"

"I'll teach you sometime. Believe me, you'll notice the difference in taste."

She took a sip, wondering about his motives. "You're going to teach me soccer and how to make tea the British way? Sounds like you're planning to stick around."

"Would you like it if I did?" he asked, touching her hand.

She set her mug on the table, cupped her palms around it and didn't look at him.

"I don't know how to answer that, Sam."

"How about the truth?"

He gently lifted her hands into his and Mariella began to tremble.

"I don't know. It's too soon to say, and I don't understand why you are asking me."

"Maybe I'm just looking for a reason to stay in Bay Point. You can be that reason."

Mariella felt her heart fill with hope, but she still had to be careful. If he wanted the truth from her, she deserved the same.

"Who called you on the phone tonight?"

Sam sat back, and her hands slipped from his. The night breeze came through the window, almost extinguishing the red peppermint-scented candle on the table. Though he didn't seem shocked by her question, he watched the flame flicker before answering.

"My agent. He and my mother are both pressuring me to return home, right after the season ends."

She faced him and raised a brow. "Do they realize the season is just beginning?"

"They believe in planning for the future."

His grim smile noted he wasn't happy about the intrusion.

"And your agent?"

"Niles just wants my money."

She leaned over and blew out the candle, wishing his mother and his agent would both go *poof*.

"And you don't want to go back?"

"I'm not sure. It's too early to tell." He paused as if measuring his words. "You see, I came here for the wrong reasons, and now I want to stay for the right ones."

Mariella's ears perked up. Was it because of the injury to his knee? In her view, the aftereffects were barely noticeable. He hadn't limped at all during the barbecue. Or was it something else?

Not sure she wanted to know the answer, she pushed her mug away, and the contents slopped over the rim. She grabbed a rag from the sink, mopped up the spill and remained at the counter when she was done.

"How will you know?" She bit her lip as he got up and joined her.

Sam tapped his forehead to hers, and she held her breath as he looked deeply into her eyes.

"It's all going to depend on you."

"Me?"

"On whether you'll let me kiss you again. This time, with no interruptions."

He traced her hairline with one finger, and his nearness made her shiver with anticipation.

"No interruptions?"

He shook his head and cupped her face in his hands as if he was handling something exquisite and fine.

"Ever since we met, I haven't been able to stop thinking about you, and I don't know what to do about it."

His voice sounded tortured, and sent a tingle down her spine.

"You didn't have to come back here tonight," she whispered. "But I'm glad you did."

Sam pulled her close and she leaned her head against the warm, hard ridge of his collarbone. She could feel the solid length of his desire against her belly, and her knees went weak.

"Maybe if I kiss you, just once more, for good luck, I can walk out of here and we can just be friends."

Mariella lifted her chin. "Why don't you try it and see?" she challenged, looking deeply into his eyes.

Sam touched his nose to hers, and she felt prickles of pleasure as the tip of his tongue darted into the hollows at the edges of her mouth.

She pursed her lips, and as he licked the delicate bow in the middle, she opened them and sucked in his tongue.

Little by little, she took his flesh into hers, enjoying his groan of delight as she wrapped her arms around his neck, and tasted hot, unrelenting need.

He backed her up against the counter and broke the kiss, burying his head deep into her neck, licking her there into submission. His tongue lapped at her skin, slow and sensuous, and she swore she could feel every one of his taste buds on her skin.

Mariella mewed low and curled into him, tilting her pelvis forward, trying to get as close as possible to the hard bulge pressing against her.

The breeze blew through the kitchen, cooling the wet skin of her neck, and she leaned away, shivering. He opened his eyes briefly, and then captured her lips again.

She pulled him closer, resisting the urge to roll her abdomen back and forth against him. Doing so would put her over the boiling point, yet doing nothing made her head swoon with desire.

Let him know you want him.

With a low moan, she cleaved her mouth to his with no shame. Her mind whirled away any fear as their embrace deepened.

Let him know so he'll never forget.

They kissed for a long moment, and then she broke contact. She leaned her elbows back on the counter and opened her eyes. There was a thin veil of sweat on his forehead as Sam stepped forward, ensuring there were no gaps between their bodies.

"Where are you going?" he muttered thickly.

"Well, Coach Kelly," she murmured, looping her hands around his neck. "What's the verdict?"

"First, kissing is one thing I don't have to teach you."

Mariella smiled and nuzzled his bottom lip with the tip of her nose. "And the second?"

"I want to kiss you more."

She laughed and he brought his lips back down to hers, but she dodged the kiss, and sank her mouth into the side of his neck.

Mariella inhaled his scent, mild soap with hints of smoke from the barbecue. Without warning, her tongue darted out from her mouth to taste his skin, and she felt his stomach cave in. To know she could shock him, could control him somehow, gave her a boost of pleasure in her loins.

"Woman, you don't know what you're doing to me," he groaned.

He lifted one hand to her right breast, making her mouth water. The fabric of her dress and her silk bra underneath were thin, and her nipple puckered to life at his touch.

Sam whistled low. "But I can feel what I'm doing to you, baby."

Breathing hard, he flicked his thumb over the large, tight nub. Her arms went slack at her sides and she gasped when he pinched it and held on for a few seconds. He tugged her nipple gently toward him as if he wanted to see if it would puncture right through her clothes.

Mariella traced the tight cords of his neck with her nose, disoriented with pleasure, as he cupped and lifted both of her breasts in his hands. Drawing a tortuous circle on each nipple with the pads of his thumbs, she became conscious of the dampness between her legs.

It was clear he meant to drive her crazy. She licked at his mouth, taking great care at stroking his lips with her tongue. Laying her cheek against his, she brought her hands around to his back and began to massage the thick muscles there. She felt his body relax into hers, and his low grunts echoed into her ear.

This is madness, she thought, as he kissed her again, even more urgently than before. And she tried to keep up with his heart-pounding, pent-up passion. Her body alert to the hardness of his, she clung to him as their tongues competed for purchase within each other's mouths. Through the haze of their kisses, she suddenly pushed him away.

"Hey, what's wr—?" Sam asked, eyes glazed over.

She shook her head wildly, turned toward the window and pulled at the front of her dress, hoping that was enough to force her nipples back to a normal state.

Before she was…before they were…

"Mom, I'm hungry. Are there any leftovers?"

Caught.

Mariella heard her son's approach before he even stepped into the room. As he did, he let out a small gasp of surprise and Sam whirled around.

"Coach, what are you doing here?"

She turned on the faucet and washed her hands. "He forgot his phone here earlier, so he came back to get it."

Sam glanced over, picking up her implied cue, and pulled his phone from his right pants pocket. "Got it now. See you both at the game tomorrow."

"See ya, Coach!" Josh said before heading straight to the refrigerator.

Mariella waited until Sam left, and then locked the kitchen door. Leaning against it, she exhaled and thanked God for two things: leftovers and the squeaky third step on the staircase.

Chapter 6

Mariella leaned back against the headrest as she waited for Josh, debating whether to shut off the holiday music on the radio.

When he was younger, they'd always sung Christmas carols together, mostly when driving back home to visit her parents. The practice continued even when he became a teenager. It seemed to be the one time of year where he let down his inhibitions.

The bike accident had changed him, and made him more wary and cautious of everything, including being himself.

She couldn't blame him for feeling that way. A serious accident could change one's perspective of the world. It was like having a broken heart, and trying to make sense of what happened, even as you were healing from it.

A little Bing Crosby could help, she mused. The radio station was playing the crooner's greatest hits, so she let it stay on. Maybe the music would encourage Josh to try on a more festive mood.

He was upset with her because he wanted to go with friends to the game, but she'd insisted on driving him. It was their tradition, she told him, and besides, this was his last "first" game of high school soccer. He could celebrate with his buddies afterward, while she tried to figure out how to remove Sam Kelly from her mind.

Or how to get him into her bed. That was far more interesting.

She shivered and decided against opening the window, as the weather had turned chilly. Early-evening temperatures were forecasted to dip down into the low fifties, perfect weather for a soccer game.

To beat the chill, Mariella had chosen a red turtleneck, topped with a cream angora vest, skinny black jeans and her favorite black ankle boots. She couldn't wait for Sam to see her outfit, although she knew he'd probably be totally focused on the game.

As he should, she thought, covering a yawn. He shouldn't be obsessing over almost getting caught in the heat of passion with the mother of one of his team members.

She thought about it enough for them both. With surprisingly little regret.

Sam awakened illicit, hidden desires she didn't know she was still capable of feeling. Most of her previous dates had never gotten that far because she wasn't that attracted to them. The ones that did ended badly, mostly due to the grief she felt over her husband's untimely death.

Lust was fast and fleeting, and much easier to justify, but Mariella often wondered if true love was worth it. The deeper past hurts were, the more pain an individual could potentially inflict on a tender heart. As a widow, Mariella knew loving someone didn't rule out the fact that one day you would still be alone.

She turned her head and looked out the window. Even if it was possible, she believed pursuing a relationship with Sam right now was the wrong move. The next few months would be stressful enough without trying to parse out her feelings for Sam. The college application process, plus her PTA duties, would take up her limited free time.

Her son was growing up, becoming a man. Maybe he could handle it if she had a relationship with his coach, but she didn't dare take a chance.

Josh got into the car and shoved in his bag. Mariella jumped in her seat, so lost in thought, she didn't even hear him open the door.

"A little warning next time, please! You scared me half to death." She started the ignition and backed out.

"Wake up, Mom. The first game hasn't even started."

He smirked, but his mood seemed brighter as if he'd forgotten about their earlier argument.

"I've never fallen asleep at any of your games."

She gripped the steering wheel with both hands. His excitement was palpable and she didn't want to ruin it. She wasn't going to ask if he was nervous; she had that one covered, too.

"Then how come you never know what's going on?"

She smiled at his good-natured ribbing. "I know enough to know when you win or lose, don't I? I'm there to support you. I don't need to completely understand every aspect of the game."

He ran his hands over his uniform shirt, straightened his shorts over his thighs and then pulled at his gold soccer socks.

"If Dad was alive, I bet he would know everything about soccer."

She didn't know why he was bringing up his father now, but his words made her heart hurt. A strand of hair had loosened from her casual updo, and she tucked it back into place to distract herself from the pain.

"I'm sorry, Josh," she said, glancing over quickly.

"Forget about it," he replied in a clipped tone. "It doesn't matter."

But she knew it did, and there was nothing she could do about it. By not dating because of a few sour experiences, she'd backed herself into a lonely corner, and denied Josh the chance to have a stepfather. It wasn't fair to him.

"Why don't you ever talk about Dad?"

Mariella sighed and turned off the radio. Bing Crosby couldn't get her out of this one.

"I guess because I'm afraid if I talk about him, you'll be sad."

Josh rolled his eyes. "Mom, I can handle it."

The years without Jamaal hadn't wiped away the memories of her first love.

"We married young. He enjoyed football, so I bet he would have felt the same about soccer, too. It just wasn't as popular back then. He was smart and kind and just a wonderful guy."

Josh frowned. "I don't remember him at all."

"You were only three when he died." She reached over and squeezed his hand. "Your dad would be so proud of you now. I just know he would be."

But Josh wasn't listening. Instead, he was pointing at the windshield. "Mom, here's the school."

Mariella had been so engrossed in the conversation she'd almost driven by it. She made a quick right turn and parked the car as close to the field as possible. From her space, she could see the bleachers were already three-quarters full with people waiting for the pregame show by the school's marching band.

"Good luck! I love you."

But Josh had already grabbed his bag and slammed the door. The harsh sound was a bookend to the conversation, and a painful fact.

Nothing she could ever say or do would ever make up for the hole in her son's heart, or the time missed with his father. It was something she would have to live with for the rest of her life, and so would he.

Sam stared openmouthed at the red numbers on the scoreboard, and then at the boy who was at fault. Josh had made a stupid mistake that had cost the team the home opener.

His other players hadn't done their best, either. He wanted to rage and scream with frustration, but he knew he couldn't do that to a bunch of emotionally sensitive kids, even though they sometimes acted like spoiled brats.

He shook his head, knowing if he took a time machine back to his teenage years, he'd probably acted the same way.

The pit in his stomach seemed to widen by the second as the sense of defeat settled in. Losing was never easy, and he'd expected it to feel the same as when he was playing pro.

But it didn't.

It felt worse, and as coach he knew he had to take some, or maybe even all, of the blame.

Sam glanced back at the bleachers. He'd spotted Mariella as soon as she arrived. She'd been happy and smiling, and he remembered the twinge of pleasure in his gut when she'd waved to him.

Now her hands covered her mouth in shock as the other parents glared at her with angry looks on their faces. They were likely the ones who tried to do his job from the stands, who railed against him, too. He felt a strange sort of solidarity with Mariella, even as he wondered what the hell had happened to her son.

The opposing team was cheering, high-fiving and celebrating their win while his players stood around no doubt wishing they could slink off the field.

The referee blew a whistle, bringing the Titans coach and players out of their funk.

Both teams hustled to form a line in the middle of the field, and then proceeded to slap hands hung low, in a show of sportsmanship no one on his team was feeling, including him.

But that was how the game was played. You won, you lost and you played the next one.

Sam blew his whistle. "Huddle up on the sidelines!"

When everyone had assembled and formed a misshapen circle, he took a deep breath and spoke, trying to portray a sense of confidence he really didn't feel.

"Team, this was a tough loss for all of us. But the only thing we can do is to learn from it and move on. And that's exactly what we're going to do."

"I'm sorry, Coach," Josh choked out, sounding as if he was holding back tears. "I don't know what happened out there."

"I know what happened. You lost us the game, you numb-nut!" Dante shouted. "If you had passed the ball to me, instead of trying to take the shot yourself and be the hero, we would have won. Instead, you're a loser."

"Stop it, Dante," Sam said sharply. "We're all losers today. We win as a team and we lose as a team."

He pointed at his players with his clipboard, making eye contact with each one.

"Each one of you has something you can improve on, and believe me, I'll be dissecting everyone's performance in this game like a Thanksgiving turkey."

Dante shook off the arms of his teammates and stood in front of Josh with his fists clenched.

"You're wrong, Coach. I'm not a loser. Not like this guy," Dante shrieked, poking Josh in the chest. "He doesn't even deserve to be on the team."

"Get out of my face, man!" Josh warned through clenched teeth. "Get out of my face!"

"Josh!"

Sam turned his head and saw Mariella cupping her hands over her mouth and screaming.

"Josh, don't!"

He turned back just in time to see Dante push Josh to the ground. Josh quickly rebounded and took a swing at his teammate. Like his goal, the punch missed, but that seemed to anger Dante even more.

Sam wedged himself between them. "Hey! Break it up!"

Despite his efforts, a second punch connected, and Sam heard cartilage crunch. Blood spurted from Josh's nose.

The two boys stepped around him and kept swinging at each other.

Sam couldn't believe this was happening.

When he was playing pro, fights in the stands among fans were commonplace, sometimes turning into dangerous melees. But on the field, no matter how he and his teammates felt about each other, they never would have dared to take a swing. They respected and supported each other. Besides, if they didn't, their coach would have had their balls in a sling.

"Break it up, I said!"

He grabbed them by their sweaty collars and pushed them onto the bench, one at each end.

"Take a seat, and learn to love it. You'll both be here for the next game. Maybe two."

Soon Dante was surrounded by a semicircle of friends.

Josh, on the other hand, was alone, his nose bleeding heavily.

Sam felt a twinge of pain in his heart for the kid. Someone should have been supporting him, but it looked like most of them had taken Dante's side, while the others looked like they just wanted to run away.

In his white button-down shirt and black dress pants, he felt more like a principal than a coach and he cursed inwardly. With one lousy loss and a lame fight, the dynamics of his team were broken. He would fix it, no matter what it took, but wished there were a playbook for coaching teenagers.

He flipped his gold paisley tie over his shoulder before stooping to examine Josh's injuries. He was bent over and looked like he was about to puke.

"Can we get some help over here?"

A medic, who had been in the process of packing up, grabbed his treatment bag and rushed over.

"Who's hurt?"

Sam got out of his way. "Um…the kid with the blood?"

"I know." The guy laughed. "I was just trying to lighten the mood."

Sam scowled, in no mood for jokes, and was about to tell the man just that when Mariella rushed over.

She knelt at her son's side, but turned back and spoke to Sam. "Oh, my God. I saw him getting hit. Is his nose broken?"

"I—I don't know," he stuttered, not liking the anger he saw in her eyes.

The medic wrapped a towel around an ice pack and gave it to Josh. "It doesn't appear to be, but I advise an X-ray just to be sure."

Josh lifted his head and snuffled. "Mom, chill out. I'm okay."

Leslie swooped in, and Sam was reminded of a vulture

circling the dead. He didn't remember seeing her in the stands, but he'd heard another mom saying that the woman rarely paid attention to the action on the field, preferring to people-watch and gossip instead.

"Dante, how about you? Are you okay?"

Mariella turned and glared over her shoulder at Leslie. "Of course he is," she said in a curt tone. "My son is the one who's hurt, or didn't you notice all the blood?"

Leslie folded her arms across her Titans T-shirt. "It was pretty clear from the stands that it was your son's fault."

Mariella stood up and the two women began to argue. It was clear from their rising voices that things could escalate even further if he didn't step in, once again.

He waved his hands in the air. "Time out, ladies. I've already had to break up one fight. I don't want to have to break up another."

Leslie flashed a quick smile. "I don't know about her, but you won't have any trouble with me, Coach. Can I collect my son now? My husband is waiting for me at home."

Sam nodded and wondered why the man hadn't shown up at the game. In fact, he'd never even met him.

More parents arrived to pick up their children, and from the looks on their faces, they weren't happy with him, either.

He backpedaled a few steps and clapped his hands to get the attention of his team.

"Everyone is excused except Josh, for obvious reasons. I'll email you guys a link to the footage of the game tomorrow morning. At practice on Monday, we'll talk about what happened and how we can *all* improve our game."

It didn't take long for everyone to gather their things and leave. He was surprised no other parent chewed his ear out, but he supposed he'd have a few emails waiting for him when he got home.

Mariella walked over to him. "Coach, can I talk to you?"

He raised an eyebrow at her professional tone. After what they'd shared last night, he'd expected something a little warmer.

With a sigh, he followed Mariella downfield, out of earshot of Josh and the medic, who, although he was annoying, had managed to stop the bleeding.

She whirled around. "Why did you let this happen?"

"What are you talking about?" Sam stepped in close, to further ensure nobody could hear them.

"I saw Dante push Josh first, and you did nothing to interfere."

"Josh got in his face, too," he added.

Her mouth dropped open. "It sounds like you're blaming him. This wasn't his fault. It's yours."

He raised his palms to stop her verbal assault, even though he knew she was right. "Everything happened so quickly. I stopped it as soon as I could."

"Not soon enough," she said, spitting out the words. "Now my son possibly has a broken nose. He's been through enough pain, Sam."

He tried to touch her elbow, but she pulled away.

"Leave me alone. I have to take Josh to the emergency room."

Mariella stalked away, and then without looking back, she and the medic helped her son off the field.

Watching them go, he realized that due to the fight, there was no way he could make Josh team captain, and Dante was no longer an option, either.

"That's going to go over well with the PTA moms," he muttered.

Sam walked back to the bench and his knee started to throb. He grimaced as he hefted his equipment bag over his shoulder. Somehow, he'd figure out a way to get back into Mariella's good graces. Turns out his old coach wasn't the only one who could put his balls in a sling.

Josh pressed the ice pack against his nose and snuffled. "I ruined everything."

His voice sounded like it was swathed in cotton, but the dejection in his tone hurt Mariella the most. It made her wish she could turn back time.

"Only your shirt," she joked. "I'll have to deploy my superhuman laundry skills to clean that thing."

"Mom!" he moaned, splaying his legs across the kitchen floor.

"I'm just kidding," she said, skirting around them. "You didn't ruin everything, Josh. You only made a mistake."

He leaned his head on his arm. "Doesn't matter. Everyone hates me."

Mariella rubbed her hands over her eyes, wishing she could just lie down, but not daring to yawn because she knew Josh would take offense. She needed coffee, strength and Sam, but right now she had none of those.

They had waited for over an hour in the emergency room at Bay Point Community Hospital before being seen by a doctor. Telling the intake coordinator she worked for the mayor had not gotten her any special consideration or preferential treatment. In fact, she wondered if it had lengthened her wait instead.

"Josh, eat."

A slice of pizza lay on his plate. He pushed it away. "I'm not hungry. I couldn't taste it anyway."

The X-rays had revealed his nose was intact. He would have some pain for several days and would be practically living with an ice pack on his nose for the next few hours.

"At least it's not broken," she reminded him.

Josh picked up the nose brace that would protect him while he was practicing and waved it in her face.

"You really expect me to wear this thing?"

"Yes," she said firmly. "Just think of it as battle gear."

"Battle is right." He snorted and then squinted in pain. "When I see Dante, I'm going to—"

She slapped her hand on the table so hard the salt and pepper shakers tipped over.

"You aren't going to do anything."

He slumped farther down in his chair. "If I had my old crew, they'd have my back. They'd do something."

The group of boys Josh grew up with was part of the reason why she moved. As they got older, many of them had gotten involved in petty crimes, and she didn't want Josh to fall in line with them.

"You've got *me*, Josh. You don't need them."

She knew the statement was futile, but she said the words anyway.

"Don't tell me what or who I need. We never should have moved here!"

He ran out of the room and up the stairs, making all the stairs creak with his stomping, not just the third one.

Mariella sank down into one of the kitchen chairs, her exhaustion complete. She started to reach for a piece of pizza, and then buried her face in her hands. Her stomach in knots, she wasn't hungry, either, and always felt this way after an argument with Josh.

Her son was crushed that he'd cost his team the game, and the nose injury just made things worse. She didn't think he would quit, but she didn't rule it out, either.

It would sure make things easier for her if he did.

She'd never have to see Sam again.

Sam sat in his SUV, across the street from Mariella's house, debating whether to get out and knock on the front door. This time he was certain he wouldn't get a warm welcome.

He swore silently. The twinkling lights on the mani-cured hedges reminded him of last night, when he'd first kissed Mariella. He didn't believe in letting arguments fester, but it was too late to apologize now.

He crooked his elbow against the door. So why was he here? He wasn't the kind of man to make a fool of himself for a woman. Or at least he didn't used to be.

The lights went out in the living room, and then a few minutes later one light went on in what he assumed was a bedroom upstairs. She was going to bed and he'd missed his opportunity, though she probably wouldn't forgive him anyway.

As he drove away, he wondered if Josh would be at practice on Monday, or if Mariella would force him to quit the team because of him. The season had gotten off to a rocky start, and if he couldn't see Mariella, at the very least on the sidelines, this was going to be the longest four months of his life.

Chapter 7

Mariella clicked the alarm on her car and took a deep breath, grateful to be out in the fresh air instead of in the office. She'd left work a few hours early to attend a meeting with the principal and athletic director about the condition of the soccer field.

Leslie had texted her earlier in the day. Mariella didn't ask, nor did she care, why she couldn't be at the meeting.

Whenever she thought about how the woman had blamed Josh for the altercation between their two sons, she seethed inside. The less she had to interact with Leslie, the better, though with the number of PTA events planned for the rest of the school year, she couldn't avoid her forever.

She headed toward the school entrance, ignoring the butterflies fluttering in the pit of her stomach. When she got there, she pressed a button by the door, gave her name and waited to be buzzed in.

Sam would be at the meeting, too. She hadn't seen or

heard from him since the first game, and there was another one that night. She'd hoped he would contact her and try to smooth things over, but he hadn't and that hurt more deeply than she'd expected.

Despite her feelings, she knew how to keep it civil. In her official capacity as PTA vice president, she supported his idea for artificial turf. Not for him, she vowed, but for Josh and the rest of the kids on the team, and those who would play after them.

It was just hard to stop hoping he could be more to her than just her son's soccer coach.

Mariella's nose wrinkled at the clean but strong scent of industrial bleach in the hallways. The churning in her stomach worsened with every step.

She reached the school office and the secretary led her down a hall to the conference room. Her breath caught in her throat when she saw Sam already there, waiting. The principal and athletic director had not arrived.

Sam stood as she entered the room, but she refused to meet his eyes. She felt like royalty when he pulled out the chair next to his, even though she figured he was just being polite again. He waited until she sat down, then followed suit. They declined the secretary's offer of something to drink, and she left the room.

Mariella stared at the white wall in front of her. Out of the corner of her eye, Sam seemed uncomfortable. He tugged at the collar of his Titans sweatshirt.

"The mayor let you out early, huh?"

"When Gregory found out about the meeting, he was all for it," she replied without a smile.

"Thank you for coming," Sam said quietly. "Leslie isn't here and I wasn't sure you were going to show up."

"It's my duty as PTA vice president."

He gave her a mock salute. "Is that the only reason you're here?"

She shot him a look. "Yes. Shouldn't it be?"

"I don't know. I only hoped that—"

"What?"

"That you wanted to see me, too."

She crossed her arms in a show of defiance.

"Do you think I've missed you?"

"My ego wants to say yes, but my heart isn't sure. Except for one thing," he added.

"What's that?"

The little smile on Sam's lips threatened to melt her defenses.

"That I've definitely missed you."

He reached a hand under the table and stroked her knee. "You look beautiful today."

Defenses melted.

She touched the lapel of her custom-made gray pant-suit, paired with a silk, sleeveless ivory tank. She'd spent a small fortune on the garment in Beverly Hills, so she only wore it for interviews or important meetings.

She batted his fingers away. "Shh. I hear voices."

Seconds later Principal Desmond Taylor, followed by Brian Putnam, the athletic director, entered the room.

They all shook hands, and the two men settled into their seats.

"Before we get started," Principal Taylor said, "I'd like to express my thanks to you, Sam, for traveling all the way from London to coach the boys' soccer team this season."

"It was an honor to be invited," Sam said. His regal voice sounded humble. "Five regular season game wins so far and only one loss shows just how talented the boys are."

Principal Taylor adjusted his navy blue tie and cleared

his throat. "We also appreciate the fact you took the position with no pay."

He turned to Mariella. "As a member of the PTA board, you are aware how budget-strapped we are. Because of Sam's generosity, the only cost to us is the rent on his apartment."

"Sam's experience and expertise are invaluable," Brian added. "He's taken a load of worry off my shoulders."

She heard through the grapevine that Brian had separated from his wife over the summer. He'd found her in bed with another man and was now even more consumed with his job than ever before.

Mariella nodded, and shot a quick smile at Sam.

"My son, Josh, has already learned so much from Coach Kelly. I do want to apologize for his involvement in the altercation after the first game."

"I appreciate that, and would expect the same from Leslie," Brian said. "Will she be joining us today?"

Mariella shook her head. "She declined the meeting."

"That's too bad."

Sam folded his hands on the table. "If you recall, Josh and Dante sat the bench during the second game, and I believe they learned a valuable lesson. Sportsmanship before, during and after a game is crucial to a winning team. Titans are supportive of each other, no matter what."

Principal Taylor smiled in agreement and then glanced at the clock on the wall. "Let's get started because I know Coach has a three-thirty start time for practice."

"Thank you." Sam cleared his throat. "Although I'll only be here a few months, I feel it's important to let you know the concerns I have about the soccer field."

"We keep it mowed and fertilized, don't we, Brian?"

"Yes," Sam interrupted, acknowledging Brian's nod.

"But there are ruts and bumps from years of abuse. It's simply not safe."

"He's right," Brian said. "Coach Lander took the lead on making sure the field was well cared for, but since his illness, the conditions have declined. I also pulled a report on the monies we've spent on maintaining the current field over the past three years."

He passed out copies to the group. "As you can see, costs have been growing exponentially. Currently, we don't have enough money in the budget to give the lawn appropriate care."

Mariella traced one of the graphs with her finger. "Hmm…costs go up even as conditions continue to deteriorate. Why is that?"

"I had another landscaper, a friend of mine, evaluate the field as a favor to me," Brian said. "His conclusion is that the drought conditions we've experienced over the past few years in our area have damaged the soil. Reseeding, season after season, has rarely worked and is a waste of money."

Sam jumped in, addressing Principal Taylor. "An uneven field can cause undue stress on the body, and even cause serious injury. It's like a ticking time bomb just waiting to go off." He handed the report back to his boss. "I recommend we replace the existing field with artificial turf as soon as possible."

"I agree with Coach," Brian said. "It's only a matter of time before someone gets hurt."

"What's all this going to cost?" Principal Taylor asked, staring hard at the two men.

Sam furrowed his brow. "I'm not sure, as I've only played on these fields for most of my professional career. I've never been involved in the transition over from grass to turf."

The principal steepled his fingers. "But I assume you'd

know what to look for in terms of quality? Good turf versus bad turf?"

"Of course." Sam nodded. "I'd be happy to help evaluate samples and choose a vendor."

"I can call other athletic directors and soccer coaches I know in the region and get recommendations," Brian offered. "This won't be a difficult task."

Principal Taylor leaned back in his chair and huffed out a breath. "But paying for it will be. We cannot ask taxpayers to do more than they are already."

"I did some research this weekend," Mariella piped in, and three heads swung toward hers. "There are grants available for this type of work. Once we select the vendor, I'd be happy to help write up our application."

"Oh? I didn't know you did that kind of work, Mariella," Principal Taylor said.

She fought the urge to roll her eyes, not believing he hadn't heard about her recent efforts for the betterment of Bay Point.

"So far, I've written two grant proposals for the city. You know the new steps going down to the beach over at Xebec Crossing? It was paid for by a grant I wrote, and I also worked on one for a new playground."

"You're hired!" the principal called out and everyone laughed.

"The PTA can help with fund-raising, too, to help defray the costs," she added.

They discussed a few more details as a group before adjourning a few minutes earlier than expected. After they all said goodbye, the athletic director and the principal stayed in the conference room for another meeting.

Mariella was silent until she and Sam were outside the school entrance.

"Good meeting, wasn't it? Sounds like you're going to get what you wanted."

"Not everything I want," he said. "I'll walk you to your car."

"You don't have to, Sam," she demurred. "I don't want you to be late."

"Start walking," he said, smiling, "and I won't be."

They moved toward the parking lot. She clasped her hands behind her back and glanced over at him. "I meant what I said back there. Josh loves soccer, but he seems to love it even more now that you are here."

He shrugged. "I'm not used to being a coach, and I'm still learning the best ways to deal with the kids and their parents. Both can be very temperamental."

Mariella smiled encouragingly. "You're doing fine, and like the principal said, everyone appreciates you."

"What about you? How do you feel about me?"

She looked straight ahead, her throat tightening. "I like you, just like any other parent would."

"That's not what I meant. How do you *feel* about me?"

"I don't know, Sam," she replied, bowing her head.

He stopped short just before they reached her vehicle. "Why don't we meet off the field and figure it out together?"

She turned toward him, wanting so badly for him to kiss her, but they were still on school property.

"Where and when?"

"I'll text you the details later tonight."

Mariella leaned against her car in disbelief. Sam Kelly had just asked her out on a date.

Sometimes it pays to eavesdrop.

Sam spread a thick blanket on the warm sand at Coquina Cove, and set a picnic basket on top.

As soon as he'd heard about the so-called private spot on Bay Point Beach from conversations at Ruby's Tasty Pastries, the local coffee shop, he knew he had to experience it himself.

Glancing up at the sky, he smiled. It was just after 8:00 p.m., and the sun was already half-set, with hues of red and orange mixing with the dark blue of twilight. *Perfect for seduction.*

He had a sensual image of Mariella in his mind that was part of his fantasies for weeks. Knowing she would be in his arms soon made him throb with desire.

Since there was no address, he'd texted Mariella directions and the GPS coordinates. Even with that information, he'd had a little trouble locating the hideaway. Since she was a local, he hoped she'd have better luck, even though she said she'd never been to the cove before.

He peeked into the basket, borrowed from Maisie Barnell. The woman hadn't outright asked, but he could tell she wanted to know about the lucky lady at the picnic table. While he wouldn't fess up a name, he did tell her she was a Bay Pointer, to which Maisie enthusiastically applauded.

Sam could still feel the imprint of Maisie's wet kiss on his cheek. A thank-you for helping her with her mission to see all the single ladies in Bay Point married in her lifetime. A lofty goal, he thought, that some folks would even call crazy.

He didn't have the heart to tell Maisie that marriage wasn't on his mind, especially since his stay in Bay Point would be brief. Something told him the woman wouldn't have believed him anyway.

Though he didn't think his attitude was unusual, as he got older, being married seemed to be a must-have milestone. His mother griped he'd long since passed it.

His phone buzzed and he saw a text from Mariella,

letting him know she'd arrived. Access to the beach cove was gained by walking down a rocky path hidden among a dense grouping of trees. He made his way up easily, and took her hand to escort her.

Midway down, he became impatient and swept her up in his arms. Her white linen miniskirt flipped up briefly, almost exposing her underwear. He was pleased she'd dressed up for the occasion, but hoped she did it more for herself than for him.

"What do you think you're doing?" she demanded with a giggle, smoothing her skirt back down. "I can walk down on my own."

She looped her arms around his neck and nestled against him. He sighed inwardly at the feel of her warm bare legs against his arm.

"Yes, and the sun will have set by the time you get there," he breathed, already getting a hard-on.

"It's steep," she said innocently. "I was being cautious."

"And I'm just being gallant," he said, nudging her closer. "Besides, this will make up for me not picking you up at your door."

"I didn't want Josh to see you."

"I understand." He gave her a peck on the forehead. "You want me to be a secret. Your secret."

He stopped walking, leaned down and gave her long, slow kiss. When he lifted his lips, she gazed into his eyes.

"Is that so wrong?"

"Only when I want to shout to the world how beautiful you are."

The sound of Mariella's laugh rang in his ear. "Put me down, Sam."

"At your service, sweetheart."

Sam set her down with a gallant bow, admiring her red-painted toes and red leather sandals.

"Allow me to give you a tour of our dining facilities tonight." He spread his arms wide. "We have a gorgeous sunset, a warm blanket, LED candles and champagne."

She laughed and tucked her legs under her. "No turkey or pumpkin pie? It is almost Thanksgiving, you know."

He waggled his eyebrows and patted his flat belly.

"And ruin my figure? I have fruit and cheese instead."

After joining Mariella, he reached into the basket to get the food. "Any plans for the holiday?"

She took the wrap off a small bowl of grapes. "We're heading down to my parents' house in East Los Angeles. What about you?"

"I'm going to Cozumel to visit a former teammate of mine," he replied, snagging a piece of cheese from another plate. "He's living there with his wife and teaching soccer to underprivileged children."

Sam filled two plastic flutes with champagne while she took off her red leather sandals.

"So what are we celebrating?"

He raised his glass. "You. Me. The fact you're still talking to me."

"I know," she teased and took a sip. "Mmm...very bubbly."

He took a large swallow of his drink and his eyes grew serious. "After what happened at the first game, I really thought I'd never see Josh or you again."

"I admit I was really angry. But when we both calmed down, I realized how hard he's worked and how much he loves the game."

Sam nodded. "He's a talented kid. I'm just sorry I couldn't name him team captain. When I announced who it was today, he didn't seem too upset."

She put her hand on his knee. "You helped him get past his injury. That's what is most important. Did he tell you he's going to his last physical therapy appointment on Friday?"

"No, but that's terrific news."

"He has you to thank for it."

Sam finished his champagne. He lifted her hand and kissed her knuckles. "I'm sure his mother had more to do with it than me."

"Thanks. Being a single parent is hard. I've given up a lot for my son."

He nodded and drew her into his arms. "I can only imagine. Tonight is your night off. Don't think about anything."

"Hmm. You're making it too easy." She bit into a piece of cheese. "This is delicious."

Sam nuzzled his nose against her ear, enjoying the smell of her perfume.

"One other thing bothered me about that first game."

"What's that?"

"My good luck kiss didn't work," she pouted.

"Since we have another game tomorrow night, I guess we'll have to try again, won't we?"

Her good luck kiss may not have worked for that particular game, but since their time together, he'd thought of nothing else.

The fact that they'd almost been caught made it all the more exciting. If Josh had not interrupted them, he would have made love to her right there in her kitchen. On the counter, or on the floor, it didn't matter to him. He suspected that in the heat of the moment, she felt the same.

On Coquina Cove, tucked away against the cliff and shielded by its rocky overhang, they were safe from roving eyes. The location was remote and romantic, and there were no houses around as far as he could tell. But the possibility they might get caught only increased his desire for her.

"I have a confession of my own to make. I've wanted you since I saw you on the soccer field."

She finished her champagne and handed him the empty glass.

"I thought it was that day in the gift shop. Didn't my palm trees turn you on?"

"No. It was those tight little jogging pants you wore that drove me crazy." He trailed a finger down her cheek. "Or maybe it was you running around the track, always in sight, but out of reach, during the tryouts. I could barely concentrate on what I was doing. And then that night in your kitchen."

"Your accent was the deciding factor for me."

"Oh, really? Not my looks or my money?"

"No, just your voice," she teased.

His skin flushed hot when her eyes traveled up and down his body. "But I'm sure there are other parts of you that will turn me on, too."

There it was. The invitation he'd been waiting for, and needed to hear.

Sam smiled and held in a breath of relief. Her boldness seemed sincere, but he needed to ensure there was no misunderstanding on his part. He couldn't bear the thought of hurting her.

His feelings for this woman were growing complex, and would take time to sort through. Right now he just wanted to love her with his body, and worry about his heart later.

"Mariella. Are you sure?"

"Is this your British politeness at work?"

"No, I care about you. I want you to be comfortable with me, with us. I don't want you to re—"

She sat up, pressed two fingers against his lips. The tears in her eyes moved him to the core of his being.

"Shh... I won't regret this. Just kiss me, Sam, until I can't feel anything but you."

He gazed at her, giving her one last chance to push him away, but she leaned in close to him. It was dark now, and the candles made her skin glow even more beautifully.

Knotting his hand in the back of her long hair, he crushed his lips to his. There was nothing demure about the way she accepted his tongue in her mouth. She opened up as if she was starving and he was her sweet nectar, her only source of nutrients.

Her lips, so plump and eager, never departed from his as she cradled her arms possessively around his neck and pulled him closer while their kisses flourished and bloomed.

She murmured low in her throat while he tried to satiate her with warm, wet kisses that tumbled over and over. Mariella clasped his head between her hands, sucked on his bottom lip until he groaned, and he knew this time she needed more.

Laughing, she broke away, breathing heavily, and got up on her knees.

He lay down on the blanket and clasped his hands behind his head. He watched, fascinated, as her fingers slowly worked the pearl-like buttons on her red cashmere sweater. The garment slipped easily from her shoulders, revealing a red lacy bra.

Her belly, exposed and flat, served as an altar to her firm breasts, larger than he'd even imagined, as she bent over him. He remembered feeling them over her clothes in her kitchen, and his mouth began to water.

Unable to restrain himself, he propped himself up on one elbow and stole a quick lick. The fabric was rough, and her nipple bounced against his tongue, and before he could grab onto it with his mouth, she pushed him back down.

"Oh, baby, why?" he protested.

Giggling, she gave him no answer as she unsnapped the front of her bra, releasing her breasts to him. He gasped at the sight of her dark nipples, and even darker areolas, and then licked his lips. His hard-on grew in his black jeans, and he caught her eyes appraising the bulge.

She straddled him and undid the buttons of his black button-down shirt, her breasts swaying in the air above him. He hurriedly shrugged out of his shirt and tossed it to the side, then ran his hands over her curves while she moved her hips suggestively over his jeans.

He sucked in a breath as she kissed his bare skin, from his chest to the waistband of his jeans, nipples grazing a hot trail all the way to his belt buckle. With a hard swallow, he got rid of it and then his jeans and underwear, kicking them aside, too.

She let out a coo of delight as his penis sprang free, but before she could touch him, he hiked up her skirt and put his hands on her thighs. Moving higher, he touched her between her legs. Her underwear felt as lacy as her bra, but more important, the fabric was wet with her desire for him.

"Get rid of these," he grunted, and he folded his hands back behind his head to watch her strip.

Mariella shimmied out of her skirt and her underwear, and he let out a slow whistle. The wedge of hair between her legs was black and thick and wiry, just the way he liked it.

He took her hand and tugged her forward until she collapsed on him, straddling his abdomen once more.

She leaned back against his raised knees and Sam took his time exploring between her thighs. His fingers slipped easily through her silky moistness, until she threw her head back and moaned so deeply it made him tremble.

After retrieving a condom from his jeans and slipping it on, he laid her onto her back. Eyes glazed over, she reached for him hungrily. He gripped her pubic hair lightly and spread her wet flesh with his fingers, tickling her softness.

Mariella tried to touch herself, but he batted her hand away. So biting her lower lip, she spread her legs wider, teasing him with an open view. Licking his lips, he got in between her and leaned back on his haunches. She was glorious. He grabbed her hips and bent his head, wanting to taste her so badly, but knew he wouldn't be able to contain his need for her.

With a groan, Sam lurched over her, bracing his hands on either side of her head and penetrated her. He gritted his teeth and almost came instantly. She was as tight as a virgin, and her internal muscles locked onto his throbbing penis, boosting his pleasure.

As he moved inside her, Mariella's mouth pursed with pleasure and she dug her heels into the blanket. He caught one of her nipples between his lips and sucked slowly, leisurely, not willing to let go of one hardened tip for the other, even though he was sure it was just as tasty.

Before long he weakened and began to massage her other breast. She cried out as he propelled himself inside her deeper, but just as slowly, so she could feel each and every inch of him.

She thrashed her head so he caught it gently between his hands, her words unintelligible as she bucked her hips to meet his, daring him to thrust even deeper.

Releasing her hard, soaking-wet nipple, he laid his full weight upon her. Her breasts rubbed against him as they moved together. After a while he slowed down and stroked the hair away from her face. Tenderly, he kissed her neck, not quite believing he was here with this beautiful woman, who was about to be totally his.

She massaged the small of his back with the heel of her palm, a gesture that was unusual, but one he found incredibly erotic. Her feet slid up and down the backs of his legs in rhythm with his movements. With her head sandwiched lightly between his forearms, she whispered his name with every single plunge, as if she was claiming him.

Sam covered her mouth with his lips and increased his speed. Flesh slapped against flesh, the sound mixing with the waves crashing against the shore. It was a sound only for them, and he moved even faster, loving the music they were making.

Suddenly, he tore his lips away. His eyes roamed the starless sky.

Nearly overcome by the white-hot pleasure searing them both, his body stilled and he wasn't sure he could go on. He gulped in the salt-scented air, but it wasn't enough.

He wanted her.

She leaned up and kissed his chin, and he stared down at her, marveling that she was so beautifully his. He wanted to freeze his place deep inside her as he desperately tried to hold on to the last of his senses.

"Don't move, Mariella," he commanded. "I'm so close."

A bead of his sweat dropped down and trickled between her breasts. Without thinking, he licked it away and the tenuous hold he'd had disappeared.

"Me, too, Sam."

Her voice was husky. With the sexy way she lifted her hips, encouraging him to go on, he was willing to risk everything for her.

Deeper and deeper, he thrust himself into her until there seemed to be no end to the bold sensuality of her hands. Her nails sank into his skin, but he felt no pain, only that she needed him as much as he needed her. Faster and faster he moved until she began to writhe with torrid wails of pleasure he knew he would never forget.

Hot tears came to his eyes. With a loud gasp, he stilled and let go in spurts of heat. There was no time to consider the shock of his emotions, because as he cradled Mariella's face between his palms, he discovered she was crying, too.

Chapter 8

Mariella drove into the parking lot at the back of Relics and Rarities and pulled next to Sam's SUV. The large vehicle towered over her small hatchback, giving her the privacy she needed to do some last-minute primping.

Tonight was the first time she would be visiting Sam's apartment. They'd avoided meeting there because they didn't want to attract the attention of Mr. Wexler. But Sam had texted her earlier that the coast was clear, so they made a date.

She pulled out her compact, checked her reflection and liked what she saw there.

The past four weeks were some of the happiest ones in her entire life. Her feelings for Sam were evident in the glow of her cheeks and the spark in her eyes. He'd opened doors of her sexuality that had her body craving him day and night. More important, he'd opened her heart.

I'm in love.

But within her joy, sadness lurked.

Waiting to see him was the hardest part.

It seemed like she was *always* waiting.

Tonight was the last time she would see him alone for a few weeks. He planned on traveling back to London for the Christmas holiday.

A lump rose in her throat. He hadn't even left and she already missed him. Deep down, she admitted it was hard to accept her feelings for Sam because it meant one day soon, she would have to let him go.

"I'm being selfish," she said before closing her compact and tossing it back in her bag.

It was the truth, but she couldn't help it. She wanted Sam to stay in Bay Point and with her forever. And she bet if she asked every one of his team members, they would agree.

The Titans were having their best season in years. They'd won every game, except the home opener. But win or lose, each one was like a nail in her heart because as soon as the season was over, Sam would leave Bay Point and return to England permanently.

After every game she wanted to rush from the bleachers into his arms and give him a kiss of congratulations, but she had to wait until she could sneak away and see him.

Mariella dealt with the separation as best she could, and always sat in the same place on the bleachers so she'd be easy to pick out in the crowd.

He'd give her a nod and a slow tilt of a smile he'd saved just for her. The heat of his gaze would reach all the way up to the stands. When he turned back to the field, she could hardly breathe, let alone concentrate on the game.

Did he draw strength from those moments? She did, and knowing he wanted her made the waiting worth it.

With Sam in her life, she had even more confidence that she could do anything, be anything. Though he couldn't be her partner in public, she claimed him as her partner in her heart.

They never really talked about his eventual departure and she wondered why. Keeping quiet wouldn't make the truth go away. Maybe he was just as anxious about it as she.

Keeping their relationship a secret was difficult, too. She'd dreamed about making love under her Christmas tree and in her own bedroom, but that was impossible. They'd been back to the cove a few times, but stopped for fear of getting caught.

On date nights she told Josh she had a PTA meeting or was having dinner with friends. He would barely look up from his homework or computer. Lately, instead of gaming, he spent his time finalizing his college applications. He seemed glad to have some time to himself, but it didn't make lying to her son any easier.

Still, Mariella refused to feel guilty.

Every second spent with Sam was precious. Their time together was short, only a few more months, and she wanted to treasure every second of it.

They talked and texted as often as they could. Her day job and freelance grant-writing projects kept her busy enough so she wouldn't constantly obsess about him. In the past few weeks, she'd had several more meetings with Leslie and other members of the PTA regarding the new turf for the field. Several fund-raisers were being planned throughout the school year to raise monies not covered by the grant.

The danger of a damaged soccer field brought Josh's injury to her mind, as well as Sam's, and she knew she had to bring that project to a close as quickly as possible. She didn't want either of them to get reinjured.

Even as they got closer, Sam would never talk about how his injury happened. All he would say was he was still rehabbing, so she stopped asking. His knee was the only place on his body he didn't allow her to touch or kiss.

In general, he kept the details about his life in England to himself. One night he'd told her he found it difficult to trust women, based on his celebrity status and failed relationships. He asked for patience...and time.

Mariella choked out a harsh laugh. She got out her brush and stroked it quickly through her hair. Didn't he realize they didn't have any time? Maybe in his mind, their relationship was nothing more than a short-term fantasy.

A text from Sam popped up on her phone.

What are you waiting for?

She glanced up and saw him waving at her from his kitchen window. Smiling, she waved back, hurried out of the car and up the stairs.

He opened the door right away. "Something wrong with my outfit?"

Her eyes widened at the innocent smile on his face, which would be seared in her mind forever, not to mention his attire.

She burst out laughing and walked inside. After kicking the door closed behind her, she tossed her bag on the couch.

"You're wearing an apron?"

And it was one of the gaudiest ones she'd ever seen. Blueberries and cherries stuck in the middle of pine boughs splashed on a hot pink background, topped off with a white lace ruffled hem.

"I told you I was cooking tonight," he replied without batting an eye to her outburst.

Mariella molded her palms to his heavily muscled chest. "Where'd you get it?"

He winked and turned around. "Beach Bottom Gift Shop, where else?"

She gasped at the sight of his bare buttocks. *Was the man trying to drive her into a frenzy?*

"I should have known," Mariella groaned.

With a wicked grin, she lifted the hem up playfully for a peek. "I don't think it's meant to be worn like this."

"A culinary artiste like *moi* can't be distracted by clothes," he blustered.

His fake French accent sounded even funnier cloaked behind his British one.

"I must be free to move around."

"And free to love," she laughed, looping her arms around his neck. The slip of the L-word wasn't intentional, but she left it there to see what he would do.

Sam raised a brow. "Love?"

She nodded, her heart hammering in her chest as he paused a beat to gaze into her eyes.

"But dinner is almost ready," he protested mildly. "I made Jambalaya Gumbo."

Mariella peeked around Sam's shoulder. From where she was standing in the living room, she could see the kitchen, and the bedroom beyond.

She nestled her head against his chest and inhaled his masculine scent. The only thing she was hungry for was him.

"The food smells good, but you smell better. How about we cook up something ourselves? Then I can really show you how much I appreciate your artistry."

He locked the door, and then licked the deep vee of her neckline.

"Do you like my dress? It's black lace on top, black leather on the bottom. I bought it special for you."

Sam slipped his hands under her dress. "I do, but I'd rather see it on the floor."

His name caught in her throat as he suddenly cupped her bare ass. She had some surprises, too.

"Hmm," he said in a sexy tone. "Great minds think alike."

She squirmed with delight as he alternately squeezed and massaged her bare curves. Under the apron, his manhood poked and rolled against the leather. She resisted the urge to grab onto it and never let go.

"Then what are we waiting for?"

Sam ridged his teeth against the most sensitive spot on her neck until she moaned. Suddenly, he lifted her up and she clamped her legs around his hips. His penis landed between her legs, hot and long and throbbing.

He walked them both into the kitchen, and after pausing to turn off the stove, headed straight into the bedroom.

The wrought iron bed appeared to be an antique, and the room was so small it was wedged against the single window. The curtains were drawn and the only light came from the kitchen.

He tossed her down on the bed and slipped off her heels. The springs squeaked noisily as he laid his warm body on hers.

She folded her arms around his waist and started to untie his apron. "Let me help you take this silly thing off."

He reached behind and brought her arms to rest above her head, pinning them together with his one hand.

"No. This first," he whispered.

Mariella stiffened as his hot tongue dove into her mouth. Though he'd caught her by surprise with his need, soon her toes curled into the thin blanket and she was writhing beneath him.

She spread her legs, planted her heels into the blanket and dueled back, determined to prove she wanted him more. Her fingers grabbed onto the rails of the bed, wrists still bound by one of his hands.

It was the taste of him she couldn't get enough of and she stroked her tongue inside his mouth until they were both out of breath.

Sam released her wrists and stood. He lit two votive candles on the night table.

Mariella turned her face and stared, eyes wide, her fingers clinging loosely to the bed rails. His hard-on was as huge as the grin on his face.

She still had her dress on, but wished she didn't. She wanted him immediately.

"Ready to do the honors?"

He put his hands behind his head and gave a little shimmy, but his penis barely moved under the tent of his outlandish apron.

Mariella covered her face and laughed out loud at his antics. "I thought you'd never ask."

She sat up and moved slowly to the edge of the bed. Facing Sam, she parted her legs and put her feet on the worn wooden floor.

He'd joined in her laughter, but when he stared into her eyes, he knew things were about to get serious.

"Come here," she instructed.

Licking her lips, she felt exposed and raunchy as he moved toward her. The blanket felt cool and rough on her bare privates.

When he was mere inches from her face, she raised a hand and he stopped. She felt herself go wet at the pleasure waiting for her just beneath the whimsical cotton.

With a tip of one finger, she lifted the fabric, peeked underneath and wriggled slowly on the bed in anticipation.

He was harder than she'd ever seen. A long, dark slab of flesh with a hint of pink at the top. And it was all hers.

As if drawing aside a curtain, Mariella used the back of her hand to push the apron aside and over him. She watched, in fascination, a tiny drop of liquid emerge, glistening at the tip.

"Oh, my," she cooed. "Somebody's hungry."

His Adam's apple bobbed in his throat as she ran her hands up and down his back, taking her time to feel the corded muscles underneath.

"Starved," he rasped. "Take this damn thing off me."

Sam put one knee on the bed, and the mattress sank there with his weight. The one that was injured he put between her legs.

His hairy legs tickled her, and holding back a grin, she covered him up again.

"Not so fast."

Sam lifted his chin and groaned in frustration until she ducked her head under the apron. His deep sigh matched hers as she inhaled his clean, musky scent.

Under the cloak of the apron, she'd created a hot and secret place to pleasure him. His penis throbbed against her cheek as she slowly slid it against her flesh. He grunted as she sucked in his engorged length.

She grabbed onto his ass for leverage, closed her eyes and swirled her tongue around him. Once, and then a few times more.

His muscles tensed and he uncovered her head. The candles flickered, but didn't go out as he untied and threw the apron on the floor.

"I want to watch you. Loving me."

Sam's words rocked her to the core, but she could only nod. When she did, he pushed himself into her mouth a little deeper. Moaning, she accepted him and he threaded his hands into her hair.

"Baby," he breathed, elongating the word.

She tilted her eyes up and knew she had Sam under her complete control.

As she sucked and licked him, taking her time, the curtains billowed out. The briny scent of the Pacific filled the room, reminding her of Coquina Cove, where their love affair had started.

And she never wanted it to end.

He was heavy in her mouth, and her heart was thick with emotion as she tantalized him. Running her tongue and lips along his darkly veined flesh meant she was branding him as her own, even if he didn't realize it.

Mouth full with him, Mariella tentatively wriggled against his knee. She wanted to burst when her open, wet flesh made contact with a tight ridge of scars. Sam licked his lips in approval as she pleasured herself, too.

He also didn't mind when she cupped his testicles in one hand, gently manipulating them. It was the first time she'd done that, and he bucked forth, almost choking her.

She opened her mouth so she wouldn't hurt him, and he withdrew halfway before she pounced on him again.

With her every stroke, she could feel him restraining himself like a caged tiger. Her mouth felt bruised and wonderful, her nose heady with the scent of his raw desire.

"Mariella," he groaned when she took him between her lips again.

The urgency, the speed, the depth.

She held on. She controlled it all.

"Oh, God."

A guttural shout, and he gripped his hands around her face. Releasing his seed in her mouth, her head and his manhood moved as one. She held on, her arousal growing, and greedily sucked and swallowed, until he was spent.

Then she collapsed back onto the bed, the force of his climax flowing through her body. The breeze slid over her hot, swollen mouth. She slipped her dress up and over her head. Lifting her heels, she perched them on the edge of the mattress and waited quietly.

She cringed at the pop of Sam's knee as he knelt slowly on the floor in front of her, and hoped the pain in his knee wasn't bad.

He said nothing at first, but she felt his hands trembling as he began to massage her thighs.

She gasped and widened her eyes. To keep her arousal at bay, she tried to concentrate on the patterns the candle flames made on the ceiling in the dark room. But it seemed the harder she tried, the more aware she became of the way Sam was touching her.

"You're so beautiful, Mariella. My honeyed goddess."

His voice was hushed, almost in awe.

His face was close, his breath, hot waves.

And when his tongue swirled into her, it was reverent.

She arched her back from the mattress, and slowly down again to the center of his world, to his sweet tongue and gentle kisses.

Oh, how I love this man.

Mariella closed her eyes and succumbed to his ardor.

"No way we're done yet, baby."

His voice vibrated against her wet flesh, turning her on even more. She craned her head up to watch him, and when she did, he cupped her breasts.

Caressed her nipples.

One finger flicked them button-hard.

All while his tongue kept moving...darting...seeking.

He was watching her dissolve, driving her mad.

She laid her head back onto the bed. Now she was under his control, bucking her hips as he played with her, blotting away everything in her mind but him.

He moved and kissed the insides of her thighs, paying

close attention to the area where they curved down to her ass, tickling her with his lips to distraction.

"Sam, don't stop," she begged, craning her head up once more. "Go back. Love me again there, p-please."

The stark desire in his eyes brought another wave of emotion, threatening to take her places she wasn't sure he wanted to go. She wanted him to love her with his deepest self. Would that ever be possible?

He lowered his head, and she sank back down and squeezed her eyes shut. But even then she wasn't ready when he focused the tip of his tongue on her most sensitive part.

Mariella caught his head between her thighs and screeched out a moan, which soon became catlike and echoed through the room.

They were sounds she'd never made before.

A strange and primal ecstasy in their ears.

She grabbed at his hair, panting hard and at the brink. Sam gave her one final lick and wrested his head from the viselike grip of her legs.

Their bodies were slick with perspiration as he scrambled on top of her. His weight felt heavenly, possessing her. Immediately, Mariella clamped her legs around his waist, not wanting to be apart from him for a second.

Sam thrust once, his engorged thickness filling her up. He retreated almost completely and seconds later, impaled her again. And again.

"Mariella."

A short, satisfied gasp from his lips made her call out his name in ragged breaths, teased out by his ever-increasing pace.

She bit the side of his neck in shock at the force of her orgasm as they came together, moved fluidly together. His stubble scratched her jaw, and she licked his skin, tasting salt.

Mariella waited until he was snoring lightly before whispering in his ears, "I love you, Sam," hoping her words would somehow float through his dreams to nestle in his heart.

Hours later, after making love again and entwined in each other's arms, Sam struggled to stay awake. He stroked Mariella's long hair, tangled and messy around her shoulders. One lock was half-twisted around her left nipple, now softened.

He licked his lips. He knew how to make it hard again.

He also knew if he touched her again, he might never let her go home.

Sam cracked open one eye, spied the clock on the night table and sighed in frustration. It was ten o'clock. His woman had to leave very soon, and he knew she would be hurt if he fell asleep again.

His woman.

The words sounded nice tumbling around in his brain. He'd much rather Mariella stay with him, in his bed, all night, every night. But that was impossible.

Every night? He whispered the words to himself, not quite believing them. It was rare when he wanted a woman to stay with him more than a few hours, let alone all night.

I guess there's a first time for everything.

Losing sleep wouldn't be the only hazard to making love to Mariella every night. It would lift the barriers to getting emotionally close to her. He snuggled her tighter to him, knowing he was already halfway there now.

His chest heaved with anxiety. On second thought, maybe it was a blessing she had a kid.

Determined to keep both of their hearts safe from future hurt, he slid his arm away from her and swung his legs over the bed. He debated whether to ask her to join him in the shower.

"Sam, can I ask you something?"

He sucked in a breath. "Hmm?"

"How can you possibly leave me after what we just shared together?"

He turned around and stared into her eyes. "I'm leaving you? I think it's the other way around, honey, but you and I both know that's the way it has to be."

"You know what I mean," she said softly.

Yes, he knew and he didn't want to think about it.

He stood to face her and put two fingers on her lips. "Shh. Let's not ruin a wonderful evening by talking about this now."

"Why not?" She sat up and folded her arms, and he heard the impatience in her voice. "I'm tired of pretending that you going back to England isn't the elephant in the room. Don't you want to stay in America and be with me?"

Sam sat back onto the bed, his emotions mixed. For the first time in his life, he was falling in love with a woman and he didn't know what to do.

"It's not that simple."

Mariella reached for his hands, but her touch only worsened his anxiety.

"It is," she insisted. "Just. Stay."

He slipped away, leaned over and gave her a soft kiss.

"You don't understand the pressure I'm under right now. I can't just make a split-second decision. There are a lot of factors in play, including the fact that I'm just not sure I'm ready to give up on my professional soccer career yet."

"You wouldn't be giving up. You'd be doing something different."

Sam huffed out a breath. "But that's the problem. To

quit what I've worked so long to achieve...for good? To coach high school soccer permanently?"

"You act like it's been torture," she accused.

"It hasn't, and you know it," Sam said, reeling his surly tone back in. "I'm really enjoying it. The kids are playing better than ever. Best of all, we're winning."

She nuzzled her nose against his chin. "It's a testament to your coaching ability."

He felt a rush at her compliment, knowing she meant every word. Still, he didn't want her to get her hopes up.

"Maybe, but I'm not sure I've achieved all I have to accomplish in the pros."

Sam knew it was difficult for most people to fathom. There were many who dreamed of being in professional sports, not realizing the drive, effort and sheer determination it took to get there and stay there. His doctor had told him he could go back to playing pro next year, if he so desired.

He took her hand in his. "Can't we just enjoy what we have now, without worrying about tomorrow?"

Mariella sighed. "You're not giving me much of a choice, are you?"

"No, but I'll give you a lot more loving, if you'll let me." He brushed her hair away from her shoulders and trailed a finger down her chin.

"Stay a little longer, Mariella. Please? I promise I'll be the best Christmas present ever."

When Mariella smiled and took him back in her arms, Sam thought it was a fair compromise.

But even he couldn't have predicted that when she straddled his hips, took him inside her and rocked their bodies until both of their heads were banging against the headboard, that the cries of desperation would be his.

Chapter 9

The doors to the gym were thrown open wide, and teens eager for the Bay Point High Winter Dance were already trickling inside. The music was lively, a mix of Christmas music and pop tunes to get everyone in the mood for a good time.

Mariella tapped her toe in time with the music. She was in charge of one of the punch tables, and was busy arranging plastic cups in neat rows of ten. Every so often, she glanced up, hoping to see Sam.

Chaperones were expected to dress formally, and she was happy to oblige. She twisted a little so the skirt of her off-white, sleeveless, tea-length dress wrapped around her legs. In the spirit of the season, she'd pinned a large rhinestone snowflake brooch on one side.

Her ballet flats were cream-colored satin and they were so cute she found herself looking down at her feet more often than she probably should have.

More kids started to arrive so she carefully filled the cups with lemonade, trying not to spill any on the white linen tablecloths. They were on loan from Maisie Barnell, and she wanted to keep them as clean as possible.

Just as she finished, Sam walked in the door in a black tuxedo and polished black wingtip shoes.

All eyes, including hers, were on him.

He made a beeline for her table, pulling at his white starched collar. "Damn this tux. Did you ever think you'd be reliving the horrors of a high school dance?"

"Oh, it's not so bad." Mariella lowered her voice. "At least we're together."

He nodded, and his eyes roamed over her dress. The knowledge he knew every inch of her body made her quiver with desire. She still got chills thinking about the time they spent together in his apartment.

Mariella didn't know when there would be another night like that, but she was grateful just to be in Sam's presence.

Tomorrow he was returning to England to celebrate the holidays with his mother. When she asked him to chaperone the dance at the last minute, he accepted.

Strands of red and green streamers crisscrossed the gym ceiling, mimicking a glittery sky. Beautiful red and pink poinsettias, provided by Vanessa Langston, the mayor's wife, were clustered about the room and at the corners of each refreshment table.

The balsam fir trees trimmed in red and white lights with gold ribbons, donated by the city, were the prettiest decorations of all.

Mariella was proud of the efforts of her fellow PTA moms and other volunteers. She'd even been able to stomach spending time with Leslie, listening to her rattle off all the gifts she was expecting from her husband. Mariella suspected she bought them all for herself and just wrote his name on the tag, but didn't dare say that.

It was the holidays after all. Everyone had a right to indulge in a little make-believe.

She finished pouring the punch and stowed the empty containers under the table. "Let the madness begin."

"I think we both need a good luck kiss."

He touched her hand and she promptly snatched it away.

"Sam, have you lost your mind? We can't. Not here."

Mariella was grateful for the music blaring out over the deejay's speakers, which covered their conversation.

"Then I'll have to satisfy my hunger for you with a cookie."

He took one from the tray on the next table over before she could stop him.

"You're impossible," she scolded.

He took another bite and leaned over the table. "And you love me because of it."

She crossed her arms and glanced up into twinkling eyes, not sure how to respond. She hadn't told him how she felt, not directly. Had he heard her whispered devotions in his ear that night in his apartment? If so, how did that make him feel?

Shouts of laughter interrupted her thoughts and she saw that the gym was almost full. She waved at Josh, who had just arrived. He'd finally gotten the courage to ask Emily to accompany him to the dance.

Mariella shooed Sam away and he took his place near the doors.

Josh sauntered over to the table, with Emily holding on to one arm. The young woman wore her hair in a cute pixie style. Her brown eyes were shy, and Mariella was thankful her midnight-blue gown was equally modest.

She complimented the girl on her dress and then held

her arms out to her son for a hug. Surprisingly, Josh didn't shun her. Maybe he didn't want to embarrass himself or her in front of his date. Whatever the cause, she wasn't complaining.

Principal Taylor grabbed the deejay's microphone. "Teachers. Chaperones. Places, everyone!"

"Josh, we better go," Emily said, taking his hand and pulling him toward the dance floor.

"See you later, Mom."

Mariella blinked back her tears. It was bittersweet to watch her son growing up and away from her. The painful loss of her son to adulthood was tempered by her love affair with Sam. She tried not to think about it ending, too.

As the night wore on, in between filling countless punch cups, she watched Sam interacting with the students. Though the gym was crowded, it wasn't hard to keep an eye on him. He was so easygoing and handsome, many of them hovered around him, and she saw smiles all around.

Mariella wondered if Sam wanted any kids of his own. It occurred to her she'd never even thought to ask him, which intrigued and frightened her. There was a lot she didn't know about him, and time was running out to discover.

Children meant commitment, and though she loved Josh dearly, she wasn't sure she wanted another child. Next year he would be out of the house, and she would start the next phase of her life. What that would entail, she didn't know, but she hoped and prayed that Sam would be a part of it.

The dance went off without a hitch, but when it was over, it was over. The overhead lights were flipped on, and the chaperones and teachers hustled the kids out of the gym as quickly as they could, so that the cleanup crew could get started.

Leslie left soon after Principal Taylor, but nobody had

expected her to stay. She always delegated the most mundane tasks to Mariella and other PTA moms.

Mariella lost sight of Sam as she helped the team get the gym back in tip-top shape, and assumed he'd gone home.

Empty punch cups and cookie trays were dumped into the garbage. The tables and chairs were stowed away. A couple of people were wielding large brooms, with others following behind with dustpans. The maintenance crew would take care of the streamers over the holiday break.

The lights, ornaments and bows were removed and packed up. The next day a crew of PTA dads would take the decorations, along with the Christmas trees, to a few local churches and a nursing home.

The whole process took over an hour. As chair of the cleanup crew, Mariella noted that everything was done to her satisfaction and dismissed the group with her thanks.

She folded the linen tablecloths, which she would launder and iron before returning them to Maisie.

She shut off the overhead lights and closed one of the doors. The other one she left open as a reminder to the janitors to remove the garbage and take down the streamers.

She picked up the linens but they were too heavy to carry all at once, so she placed them near the door. It only took her a few minutes to walk to the teachers' lounge to get the large paper shopping bag she'd left there, so that it wouldn't get thrown away by mistake.

When she returned to the gym, Sam stepped out of the shadows.

Startled, she let the bag tumble to the floor.

"What are you doing here, Sam?" Her hand went to her chest. "You scared me half to death. I thought you were gone."

He was still in his tux, but the tie was loosened from around his neck and the top two buttons of his shirt were undone.

A slant of light coming from the deserted hallway formed a perpendicular triangle on the gym floor. He stepped into it as if it was a stage, and she could see his face more clearly. Dark shadows in the planes and something wicked in his hooded eyes.

"I couldn't leave without saying goodbye one more time."

His voice sounded haggard with need, and tears sprang to her eyes.

"Oh, Sam," she whispered. "I'm going to miss you so much."

He lifted his chin. "Come over here."

Mariella stepped over the bag and jumped into his waiting arms.

Holding her by the waist, he lifted her up and buried his face in her bosom. Wrapping her legs around him, she bit her lip as Sam pressed his mouth into her skin, dipped his tongue into her cleavage.

She felt the hard nudge of his erection against her belly as he walked them over to the gym wall. The cold concrete on her back was a sharp contrast to the heat and desire that quickly enveloped her.

His lips ravished her skin, kissing the tops of her breasts over and over. His hands molded her curves, bringing her as close as two clothed bodies could be. Her loins pulsed with need as his mouth trailed up her neck, and finally closed on her lips.

Mariella went limp and her legs slipped from his waist. As their tongues swirled together, she nearly slid down the wall until he pressed his body tightly against hers, pinning her in place.

"Sam, I—"

Her words caught in her throat when the palm of his hand scraped lightly against her breast, arousing her through the confines of her dress.

"No talking in the gym," he whispered against her mouth.

Mariella wanted to tell him she loved him, but she cleaved against him instead. His grasp around her waist was a life preserver, a heart breaker. She wanted to possess him, but she couldn't, and knew her deep emotions for him might never have the chance to be fully expressed.

She held back tears as he claimed her lips as his again. In him, in his kisses, she found heat and comfort, and a profound sense of belonging.

He broke the kiss, put his cheek against hers and began to sway.

"What are you doing?"

"Dancing," he replied, his voice hot against her ear.

She planted a kiss in the concave at the base of his neck. "But there's no music."

"You know we can make our own, my love."

My love?

Her heart melted anew at his endearment. With those words, she pushed aside any fears that what they were doing was wrong. Before she could ask him what he meant, his lips hungrily sought hers again, sending shivers down her spine.

Her heart began to pound at the thought of being with Sam right here, right now. Her desire for him blinded her to the dangerous possibilities, and also made her feel free. She wiggled suggestively against him, trying to imprint the memory of his length on her abdomen.

She moaned softly, knowing just continuing these motions would drive them both crazy, but was too absorbed by her love and her lust for him to care.

She had the vague sense that something was wrong, when she heard the low crackle of the shopping bag.

He seemed as oblivious to his surroundings as she was as he pinned her back against the wall and deepened his kiss, arousing her even more. She croaked out his name and tried to push him away, but his hold on her was too tight.

Suddenly they were bathed in light and she knew her life would never be the same.

"Well, well, well." Leslie sneered. "This is most inappropriate."

Sam's grip loosened and she slipped out of his arms, tripping over his feet in the process.

Mariella and Sam glanced at one another, both squinting under the glare, and then at Leslie.

"What are you doing here?" Mariella blinked.

She wondered how long the woman had been there, and how much she'd heard, or seen.

Leslie crossed her arms and gave her a shocked, incredulous look. "I should ask you the same thing. But I'm not stupid. I *saw* what you both are doing here."

Mariella rushed forth to try to explain, but Leslie stepped back and her heels almost got caught in the shopping bag.

She reached for it, but Leslie snatched it up and crushed it between her hands into a tight ball.

"Don't bother. Just get out."

Mariella's heart pounded with fear. She glanced over at Sam. His face was impassive and he appeared unperturbed by Leslie's appearance.

"You're not being fair," he said.

"I'm not being fair?" Leslie narrowed her eyes. "You don't have the right to say that to me. Not anymore. I came back to get Dante's uniform so I could launder it during the break, and what do I find?"

She pointed her finger at him. "You won't get away with this. Neither of you will."

"It's not Sam's fault."

Sam took a step forward. "I'm sorry, Mrs. Watkins."

Leslie backed away, like he was poison. "Apology not accepted. It's clear that you're not fit to coach our kids. I tried to give you the benefit of the doubt, but it appears everything I've read and heard about you is true. You're nothing but an international playboy."

Mariella shook her head, even though she'd once accused Sam of the same thing.

"Leslie, don't. Please. Let's talk about this."

She whirled toward Mariella and pointed at her. "And you were stupid enough to fall for it, for someone like him."

"We weren't hurting anyone, Mrs. Watkins."

"Oh no? I disagree, Coach Kelly. And so will Principal Taylor."

Mariella wanted to run into Sam's arms and defend him further, but she didn't dare. She took a deep breath to calm her racing heart.

"What are you going to do?"

"You both should have thought about that before you brought your little affair onto school grounds."

Leslie threw the crumpled up shopping bag at their feet and marched out of the gym.

Chapter 10

Mariella dug into a large bowl and started mixing the dough inside with her hands, ignoring the white cloud billowing around her elbows. She was up to her arms in flour, and in trouble. Tomorrow was Christmas and she really needed a miracle.

Ever since Leslie caught her and Sam kissing in the gym, she'd been baking. It was the only thing she could do to keep her from going mad as she waited for the phone call from the principal, demanding she resign from the PTA.

The resulting scandal could even cause Sam to lose his job, and she could also lose hers.

Over the past three years she'd worked so hard to build a reputation as a good mother and a loyal employee to the mayor. Every time she thought about what Gregory would think about her when he found out, she wanted to faint.

If Josh found out, he'd be so embarrassed he'd probably never want to go to school or speak to her again.

She was even scared to pick up the *Bay Point Courier* from her front steps, worried the headlines she might find would reveal her relationship with Sam in big, bold print.

But there were no calls and no headlines, which worried her even more.

Mariella sprinkled flour on a sheet of wax paper, and then slapped the dough on top, intending to knead all her frustration away. She'd tried humming, but even her favorite holiday carols on the radio couldn't lift her spirits.

That night they'd hustled out of the gym. Sam carried half of Maisie's linens, and she carried the other half because Leslie had completely destroyed the shopping bag.

He'd tried to reassure her and told her to stop worrying, and she accused him of being flippant about the situation. He did not try to kiss her. They got into their cars and drove their separate ways. Since then, she'd refused to talk to him and ignored all his text messages.

Perhaps it was a good thing he had gone home for the holidays; maybe then he'd realize that their relationship was doomed from the start.

Getting caught by Leslie was serious business, even if he didn't think so. The threat of a scandal was something he dealt with all the time when he was playing pro. He was used to it, which is why he could take it in stride. Mariella kneaded the dough until her fingers hurt and placed it in a bowl to rise.

"Hi, Mom."

"Josh!" she exclaimed, turning around. "Why didn't you use the back door?"

Sam peeked his head in the room, and then stepped inside. "Can I come in, too?"

"We wanted to surprise you. Coach Kelly stayed in town."

Mariella put one hand against her head, forgetting it was full of flour.

"You did?"

He gave her a casual nod. "Change of plans."

When she shot him a questioning glance, he raised a brow as if to say "we'll talk about it later."

Mariella walked over to the sink and washed her hands.

"Nice apron," he said in a humorous tone. "I would have brought mine, but I left it at home."

Her red apron had brown reindeer made of felt, prancing on a snowy hillside. Each one had a sequined green collar and tiny jingle bells. It was a tradition to wear it while she was doing any baking during the holidays.

She glanced back at him and her face heated at the admiring smile on his face. Whatever tension was between them disappeared, and the pleasurable memories rushed back. Images of their night in his apartment danced in her head.

She turned toward the window, hid a smile and did a couple of little twists.

Ring-a-ding-ding. Ring-a-ding-ding.

"Mom, please," Josh groaned and clapped his hands over his ears. "Not the bells."

She turned and caught Sam's eyes watching her body as she removed the apron and hung it across one of the kitchen chairs.

"C'mon. Where's your Christmas spirit, Josh?"

She smoothed her hands on her blue jeans in an attempt to stop them from shaking under Sam's gaze.

"It is almost Christmas, you know."

Josh unzipped his hoodie. "Duh, Mom. I was shopping for your present and my ride bailed on me. I just happened to run into Sam, and he gave me a ride home."

"I was shopping, too," Sam said, and she detected a mysterious twinkle in his eyes.

"Both of you waited till the last minute?"

"Of course," Sam said. "We're men, right, Josh?"

"Right! Mom, where's the wrapping paper? I want to wrap Emily's gift."

She thought a moment. "Upstairs in my bedroom."

Josh went into the refrigerator and grabbed a bottle of water. While his back was turned, Mariella gave Sam a shy smile.

"Okay," Josh said after a large swig. "I'm going to go wrap it up so I can take it over to her house later. She wants to put it under her tree."

"If I don't see you, have a merry Christmas, Josh."

He nodded. "You, too, and thanks for the ride."

Mariella waited until she heard Josh shut his bedroom door, and then motioned Sam to join her near the sink.

He went to her side immediately. "Heard anything?"

"No, and it's killing me." She folded her arms across her chest. "What about your boss? Did he say anything to you?"

"Right now Brian thinks I'm back in England. But I suppose he'd text if he wanted to fire me, which he won't, and neither will Principal Taylor."

"How can you be so sure?"

"Because the Titans are winning. Now, if we were losing, then I'd be in trouble."

"How can you think about winning now?" She shook her head at the smugness in his tone. "You think this is all a joke, don't you?"

He tried to embrace her, but she pushed him away.

"Don't, Sam."

She grabbed a wet dishrag and waved it at him. It was an effective weapon, and he stepped back.

"Why didn't you go home like you'd planned?"

He was quiet as she furiously wiped away the flour from the countertop. Normally, she was very accurate and neat with measuring, but not this time.

"I couldn't leave with things so up in the air."

She paused her hand. "Between us or with Leslie?"

"Both," he said with no hesitation.

"Very charitable of you."

Mariella tossed the dishrag into the sink and washed her hands again, not sure why she was in such an irascible mood.

She wanted him to get out.

She wanted him to stay.

He let out a sigh as he sat down, and when she opened her mouth to protest, her heart resisted.

Sam looked so relaxed sitting in her kitchen, so warm and cozy in his black long-sleeved T-shirt and gray stonewashed jeans, it was as if he belonged there all along.

"What's going to happen to us, Sam?"

"Nothing, I hope." He shrugged. "Maybe Leslie had a change of heart."

She rolled her eyes. "Ha. The woman doesn't have one."

Sam got up and put his arms around her waist, and she collapsed against him, no longer able to resist. Being away from him for two hours, let alone two days, was torture.

"Mariella. We weren't doing anything wrong."

"No, we were just doing it in the wrong place."

"I know," he admitted, nuzzling the top of her head with his nose. "This is all my fault. I couldn't resist you. That's why I couldn't leave you right now."

But what about later?

Mariella snuggled her cheek against his chest. She was glad he'd decided to stay in town. His apology meant he was finally taking her concerns seriously, which was a sign he cared about her. Too bad it was a little too late.

"Thanks, Sam. I appreciate it. I've been so worried about everything."

"You needn't be. I told you I would take care of you. Why haven't you returned my calls or text messages?"

She pulled away again. "Because I'm confused. Because no matter whether we got caught or not, this is wrong."

"What? Us?" he asked.

She nodded, and he pulled her to him and drew his knuckle along her jaw.

"No way. This is right. *We're* right."

Mariella shook her head and refused to meet his eyes. "Not anymore."

Releasing her, he leaned back against the counter. "What are you saying, Mariella?"

Her heart pounded in fear, but she couldn't stop now.

"I'm saying we're finished. It's been fun, but we're done."

Sam's eyes widened, and she was willing to bet this was the first time a woman had ever broken up with him, instead of the other way around.

He put his hands on her shoulders. "No. This will blow over, Mariella. For all we know, it already has."

"Maybe it hasn't." She closed her eyes, not wanting to see the defeated look on his face, refusing to be persuaded. "Maybe it hasn't even begun."

"Look at me, Mariella." He cradled her face in his hands and she opened her eyes again.

"I came back because we have something special and I want to protect it."

She fought back tears as the meaning behind his words stirred her emotions. It was true that they had something special. So special she'd fallen in love with him.

How was she going to cope without him in her life?

But she'd thought it over and firmly believed that even though it would be painful, ending the relationship was the best course of action.

There was nothing she could do about her feelings, except try to stem the tide of their passion before it crashed into her heart, breaking it and her life into a thousand pieces.

She was rooted in California, while he had traveled the world. Their paths were divergent from the start, by thousands of miles, crossing continents and time zones. They were able to bridge the divide with their bodies, connecting in beautiful, sensual ways, but that would never be enough for her.

"You'd better go now, Sam."

"Don't you want my Christmas gift first?"

She stared up at him. "You didn't have to get me anything."

He left and retrieved a shopping bag from the front entrance to the kitchen where he and Josh had entered. With great flourish, he took from it a rectangular box, gift-wrapped in shiny gold paper and white sequin ribbon, with a card stuck on top.

"Before you cut me loose forever, I want you to open this box up tonight and then decide." He lifted her chin with the pad of his thumb. "Promise me?"

She stared at the beautifully wrapped gift, terrified and curious at the same time, and tears sprang into her eyes.

"What's the point, Sam? You didn't leave for Christmas. So what? We both know you'll be gone by Easter. And now with Leslie potentially telling the world, or at least everyone in Bay Point about us, I don't see how this can solve anything."

She tried to hand the box back to him, but he refused to take it. Finally, she set it on the counter, for fear of dropping it, as he approached her.

Sam's lips were inches away from hers, hovering close enough for her to turn away, and yet she couldn't.

"Let's be candid, shall we, Mariella? You've fallen in love with me."

She couldn't deny the truth of his words.

When had he first known?

It didn't matter now. He did know, and she was blissfully relieved. Tears of happiness welled in her eyes as he peppered her nose with sensual, butterfly kisses.

"Isn't it only fair to give me one last chance to prove that I've fallen in love with you?"

Sam brushed his lips against her mouth, tapped her tongue with his, and she was gone. As their embrace deepened, they became lost in one another and neither heard the wooden stairs creak.

Sam parked his car, locked it and saw Mr. Wexler walking down the stairs from his apartment.

"Good evening, Sam. Your mother emailed me. Wanted me to check in on you. She said you were supposed to be back in London for Christmas."

He jingled his keys in his hand. "Yes, I canceled my flight and decided to stay here."

"You might want to let her know. She sounded worried."

"I left her several messages, but she tends to want proof. Hence, her sending you on a reconnaissance mission."

Wexler chuckled. "I know. She's tough. Questions every piece of Staffordshire I find for her. I'm surprised she doesn't fly over and pick them up herself."

Sam gasped half jokingly. "Don't even suggest it because she would."

"If you're going to be around on Christmas Day, Lucy's serves a nice brunch. Most shops and restaurants are closed."

"Thanks. I may check it out."

"I'd invite you for dinner at my place, but I tend to put

on some holiday music, heat up a frozen dinner and kick back with a cigar in front of a fireplace. I'm not quite Scrooge, but close."

"I'll be fine. I may head down to San Francisco for the day," he said, in an effort to get him off his back. He had other plans in mind.

"Been quiet upstairs lately. Everything all right?"

He gave the man an odd look. "Sure, why?"

"I don't have Wi-Fi at home, just here. Makes it easier at tax time. Sometimes I stay late and scour the internet for my latest treasures. My computer is in an office at the back of the shop, right under your bedroom." He flashed a wicked grin. "If it was a woman who changed your mind to stay home for the holidays, it sounds to me like she's a keeper."

Sam felt his face get hot. Wexler must have heard some of his and Mariella's most intimate moments.

He managed a grin. "You may be right, Wexler."

"Did I hear right, Sam? You're not coming back?"

"For the holidays, Niles." Sam stretched out on the couch. "Don't I even get a merry Christmas?"

He'd taken a cold shower, and gotten into his long flannel pajama pants. He crossed his bare feet at the ankles.

"Don't change the subject," his agent scolded.

"Why aren't you wearing an ugly sweater and opening gifts today?"

"Because I have no children and no life. Listen to this… 'Independent sources have confirmed Sam Kelly will be back in Brent for the holidays, and for good.'"

Sam chuckled as he brought up the front page of a popular London newspaper on his phone.

"You're quite the story spinner."

"I didn't create this one, mate. The team is really missing you, Sam."

His phone was on speaker. Sam was tempted to hit the off button, in his boldest bah-humbug move yet.

"So say the headlines."

"This time it's true."

His agent's voice sounded as if he was sitting across the table from him, not halfway around the world.

"Oh, yeah? How come I never hear from them and only from you?"

"Because they don't want to persuade you into coming back. They know that's my job."

"Judging by the scores, Team Valor seems to be doing fine without me."

"They'd be doing better with you and you know it."

Sam shrugged. "I don't know much of anything anymore."

"What's this? You sound like you've lost your best friend."

"No, only the best woman I've ever known."

"Uh-oh. What gives?"

"Why should I tell you? You're part of the problem," Sam complained, even though Niles was the most sought-after sports agent in soccer.

"I only put those stories out there to boost your playboy image. It got you tons of press."

With only one or two months off, Niles knew Sam didn't have the time for a serious relationship. Traveling allowed him to meet, and sometimes bed, women all over the world. Sam never wanted those trysts to last, nor could they. Not with his schedule.

He frowned. "I guess it served a purpose. But now that I'm over here, none of that matters. In fact, it's only hurting me."

And the woman I love.

The thought gave him pause.

Was he really truly ready to love Mariella?

"I may have gotten myself into some hot water over here."

"Eh? What do you mean?"

"I got caught kissing the mom of one of my players, by another mom, in the school gym."

Sam could almost hear the man rubbing his hands together and plotting.

"Sounds like headline material here in the UK. We appreciate a juicy scandal, especially when it involves a handsome, still single footballer, like you."

Still single.

His agent's words entered Sam's brain and stuck there, taunting him with the possibilities.

"I'm told the same is true here in Bay Point, but the mom who caught us hasn't done anything about what she saw. Yet."

"Good news, right?"

"No. The woman I was kissing won't see *me* again."

"So? You don't need to get tangled up in a relationship for more than one night anyway. It will only make it harder to leave."

"And who says I'm leaving?" Sam demanded.

"I do. Your doctor says you're recovered enough to play," Niles replied in a mild tone. "It's only a matter of time, and dollar signs."

Sam was too angry to even speak for a moment. He didn't want to even think that he was capable of leaving Mariella now, but deep down, he knew that he was.

"Forget the woman, whomever she is, and come back to England, Sam. If you won't do it for me, will you do it for your country?"

"Way to turn up the guilt, Niles. You're starting to sound exactly like my mother."

Chapter 11

Mariella had some difficulty keeping a straight face as she walked through the revolving doors of the Horizon Intercontinental Hotel around noon on Christmas day. After all the worry and angst that she wouldn't be able to see Sam during the holidays, she was on her way to his room.

The luxury hotel wasn't scheduled to open to the public until New Year's Eve. Most of the furniture was covered in drop cloths, but she didn't have to see it to know it was expensive. She'd overheard a conversation with the owner of the hotel and Mayor Langston several weeks ago. Though Gregory had no stake in the property, he'd wanted to ensure that it was as opulent as possible because he knew it would be a huge draw for tourists and A-list clientele.

Her heels tapped on the white marble floors and echoed throughout the large lobby. She bit her lip and approached the front desk, hoping the attendant wouldn't recognize her.

"I'm here to see Sam Kelly."

The man smiled and she inwardly sighed with relief. She'd never seen him around town before, and figured he was new to the area. If he thought it was strange she was wearing a raincoat on a sunny day, it didn't show on his face.

Mariella waited while he typed something in his computer. "He's in the penthouse suite."

He gave her a pass card and directions to the private elevator, and then picked up a phone call.

She made her way to the farthest corner of the lobby. As the doors closed, she tightened the belt of her raincoat, and her excitement grew as the elevator rose to the penthouse level.

Yesterday she'd waited until Josh went to bed to open Sam's gift. The handwritten card with the invitation to the hotel was a surprise, but nothing prepared her for the shock of what was inside the box.

That morning, after opening their gifts and having breakfast, Josh wanted to go to Emily's house to spend the day with her family. She was meeting him there that evening for dinner.

She stepped out of the elevator, which opened up directly in the hotel room, and looked around, feeling like a mysterious vixen in a classic film.

The place was enormous, as large as an apartment, and the furniture was plush and modern. The teak floors were polished to such a high gloss she took off her kitten heels for fear of slipping.

A slight breeze lifted her hair from where it fell softly around her shoulders. From her vantage point she could see a large balcony. The air was circulated in the room by several rustic-style ceiling fans.

Mariella stood in one place in her bare feet, not sure how far to proceed.

"Sam?"

There was only the faint sound of the ocean and then

she remembered his note. He'd been very explicit in his instructions.

Before she lost her nerve, she unlooped the thick belt of her raincoat and undid the buttons. Just before she slipped out of it completely, Sam walked into the room from an unseen entrance with a bottle of champagne, wearing nothing but a pair of black silk boxers.

She momentarily forgot to speak or where she was as she openly admired him. She thought she knew every cut of every dark bronze muscle, but in the light of the midmorning, it was clear she had a lot more to explore.

"Hello, Sam."

"I guess you read my note last night."

He bowed and it made her tremble more as the raincoat slipped from her shoulders.

Sam walked toward her, whistling low. "And you opened my gift. I need to see it from all sides."

He made a twirling motion with his fingers and she spun around.

"Baby, you look so sexy, I wish I could do backflips."

She laughed and tossed her hair. "Now, that would make for some interesting positions."

"Don't give me any wicked ideas." He grinned and held up the bottle. "I was just getting ready to open this. Want some?"

"It's never too early for bubbly."

"Let's have it out on the patio."

Her eyes widened and she crossed her arms over her chest. "But, Sam, somebody will see us."

He pulled her close for a slow, sweet kiss. "It's completely private. Just like this suite."

She bit her lip to taste him. "What about my raincoat?"

"You won't be needing it."

He grinned and led her outside. "This is the only penthouse suite at this hotel. It has two bedrooms, two baths and a full kitchen but the patio is my favorite."

Enclosed on three sides by white stucco, with its yellow-striped canvas canopy and terra-cotta tile floor, it had a very Mediterranean feel. There was a hot tub and a small pool with crystal-blue water.

"How did you get this place?" she asked, marveling at the magnificent view of the Pacific Ocean.

"I heard through the grapevine that there were a few rooms available before the official grand opening next week, so I snagged the best one. Do you like it?"

"Sam, it's gorgeous."

She crossed her arms and pointed to the small fireplace recessed into the wall.

"That could come in handy."

The temperatures were in the midsixties, under partly cloudy skies, and she was wearing next to nothing.

His gaze roamed her body. "Are you cold?"

Mariella cast her eyes downward to her black strapless leather bustier laced with grommets. She slid one of her fingers beneath her bikini underwear, the palest of pinks, in sheer chiffon. The contrast was striking and sensual.

"What do you think?" she asked with a saucy grin.

He set the bottle down on a small table next to a hammock built for two. Two glasses were already there.

"If you want me to warm you up, just say the word."

"First, pour me some champagne. I want to talk."

Mariella gingerly lay down on the hammock and accepted a glass. "We don't have much time. I'm due for an early dinner at Josh's girlfriend's house and I obviously can't go dressed in this."

"Uh-huh," he said. "That's for my eyes only."

She held a breath as Sam joined her. When she was sure the hammock could hold them both, she took a sip of champagne and rested her head back on the blue chintz pillow that stretched across the top.

"Two words. Why leather?"

He turned his head to face hers. "You look good in it. I loved that dress you wore to my apartment that night. I ordered it online and it looks like I was right about the size. Aren't you proud of me?"

Mariella gave him a kiss on the nose. "Very. I love it. This is something I never would have bought for myself."

"Get used to it. You deserve every good thing there is in this world."

His comment should have made her feel warm inside, but she only felt a sense of dread.

Sam frowned. "What's wrong?"

She drank the rest of her champagne, needing the temporary comfort it provided her.

"I'm not sure why I'm here, Sam. I was the one who wanted to end everything between us."

"Do you still?"

Mariella looked up and saw that the awning was one of those types that could be retracted into the wall. It was cozy underneath, but talking about her feelings made her feel raw and exposed.

"I don't know. I guess that's what I'm here to find out. You already know I've fallen in love with you."

"I've sensed that for a while. And I wanted to prove to you that I feel the same way, but even if I do, I'm guessing that's not enough."

She threw one arm over her eyes and peeked at him from under it. "You do realize that we don't know that much about each other, right?"

"Yes. We don't have to hide anything from each other." Sam picked up her arm and placed it on her chest. "Ask me anything."

She turned to face him. "Do you miss playing soccer professionally?"

"There are some parts I miss, others I don't."

"I want to hear all the juicy details."

He looked at her pointedly. "No, you don't."

She smiled, caught. "You're right, I don't."

"I got tired of the high expectations, the paparazzi and, believe it or not, the constant chase of women." He paused to take a sip of his drink. "I wanted a break, so I took it."

"Would you have stopped playing if you hadn't gotten injured?"

She waited while he considered the question.

"Honestly, probably not. My priorities would have stayed the same—money, fame and everything that comes with it. The injury was literally the kick that I needed to jolt my thinking and my lifestyle."

She paused, not sure if she should ask again a question they'd already hashed out. "And are you going back?"

"To England?" At her nod, he said, "Nothing has changed. I just haven't decided whether I'll continue to play professionally or just coach."

Mariella kept her face impassive, even though inside, she felt defeated at his decisive tone.

She watched the edges of the canopy snap in the ocean breeze. There was truly no chance for her and Sam to be together, but she didn't want to leave him. Not yet anyway.

He turned to face her. "I'm sorry if that upsets you."

She searched his eyes and got the sense that he wished things could be different. "It doesn't because I know it's the truth."

She took a deep breath. "I never wanted anything from you. Maybe you thought I did because of who you are, but I didn't."

Though she was careful to keep her tone light, he hitched in a breath as if he'd been punched.

"I never thought that about you."

"Regardless, it's something I've always worried about with any man. I married young, and my former husband died very young."

"I'm sorry," he frowned, stroking her arm. "I'm sure that was difficult."

She inhaled the salty air and adjusted her body more comfortably in the hammock.

"Sometimes I wonder if it was harder for me or for my son. Raising him by myself hasn't been easy."

He squeezed her hand. "You did a fine job."

"I'm not fishing for compliments, just like I'm not in the market for a dad for my son. Josh was crushed when the few relationships I have had didn't work out."

Mariella closed her eyes, remembering all the questions Josh asked her when a man she was seeing suddenly wasn't around anymore. She'd answered as honestly as his maturity at the time could withstand, but always felt bad she couldn't give him the whole picture.

"You missed having someone in your life, haven't you?"

She shook her head fiercely against what she knew was true in her heart. "A woman gets lonely, and when that happens, she can make unwise decisions. I can't let that happen again. Anyway, I think Josh has lost faith that I can ever find a man."

He laid his hand on one side of her face, and now his eyes were as tender as his touch.

"Tell him you've found one."

For now.

"Merry Christmas, Sam."

Her voice caught in her throat and she fought back tears, but not her desire, as he pulled her on top of him and kissed her.

Chapter 12

Sam jiggled his car keys in the pocket of his navy blue track pants, eager to end the day. When practice was over, he was heading straight for the gym. He glanced back at the bleachers, hoping to see Mariella, but she wasn't among the few parents who'd stopped by to watch their sons play soccer.

An old year had rolled into a new one. Today was the first day back to school and everyone seemed to have the post-holiday blues, including him.

After that day at the Horizon, he'd contacted her a few times over the holidays, but she never returned his calls.

He didn't believe in resolutions, but he'd made up his mind about one thing. If Mariella could let him go so easily, then he could do the same thing.

Or at least he could try.

He'd had plenty of practice over the years, of sleeping with a woman one night, and not calling her the next.

But he thought he and Mariella had something special together, besides mind-blowing sex. When they'd made love, she'd clung to him like a grape on a vine. He'd done the same to her.

His desire had blinded him to her fear. Normally, he wouldn't have a problem with that, but for the first time in a long time, he was in love.

Whether she was afraid of moving away from Bay Point, or moving on with him or something else, he didn't know, but she couldn't avoid him forever.

They had a meeting tomorrow with three vendors for the artificial turf project. Though he would have no part of the final selection, the athletic director and the principal wanted him there to view the presentation and ask questions. He agreed, and was glad for something to help keep his mind off Mariella and the disaster he'd made of their relationship.

Then Brian reminded him that because Mariella was working on the grant, she would be attending, too.

He checked his watch and blew his whistle three times. "That's all for today, guys. See you tomorrow."

Sam still hadn't heard anything from Leslie or anyone else at the school. He figured if he hadn't heard anything by now, he never would, so he let it pass. If he worried about every scandal he'd been involved in, real or imagined, he'd have an ongoing need for prescription anxiety pills and an attorney.

The past week he'd lain awake many nights thinking about Mariella and the trouble his lack of judgment may have caused her, and himself. He hadn't meant to be so insensitive about the situation. Mariella wasn't as thick-skinned as he was. He'd had to be, with the press and the paparazzi constantly circling around him like vultures.

Sam was beginning to wonder if he'd brought this bit of

trouble on himself as a way to get out of a relationship that was starting to mean more than anything else in his life.

A couple of the parents approached. They wanted to know if the Titans had a chance at winning the regional championship. He assured them he'd do everything possible to ensure the team maintained its current winning streak. He reminded them that much of the burden lay on the players, working together as one unit, instead of as individuals.

He thanked them for their concern and walked around the field, gathering practice balls. Here and there, he stopped in front of a clump of dirt and tapped it down with the toe of his cleats.

There was one more month of the regular season, then the playoffs, and possibly the regional championships.

Knowing he would only see Mariella in the bleachers would make every game even more bittersweet.

He spotted Josh hanging out by the goal, practicing his kicks. He was a terrific kid and he didn't want him to get hurt by their indiscretions.

It was near dinnertime. He thought about asking Josh if he wanted to join him for a slice of pizza, but quickly dismissed the idea. If the other kids or parents heard about it, he might be accused of showing favoritism.

It was better to stay clear. He would have a hard time not pressing the boy for more information about Mariella. He'd skirt around for a bit, asking him what he got for Christmas, what he did during his time off, but eventually, he'd get around to asking about his mother.

For all he knew, she was off in the arms of another man, though his heart told him she wasn't.

"Coach?"

The kid must have moved like a phantom across the field. He hadn't even heard him approach.

Sam zipped up his Titans windbreaker and whirled around.

"Josh! I saw you doing some extra practice." He gave him a thumbs-up. "Great job!"

In Sam's mind, he was one of the hardest working players on the team. By the time practice ended, he was usually the sweatiest and the dirtiest. Two tell-tale signs.

"Yeah. I was actually just hanging around until everyone was gone."

He raised a brow. "What for?"

"I saw you."

Sam felt like a rock had just dropped into his stomach. "What are you talking about?"

"You and my mother."

Josh's upper lip was trembling, even though his voice was calm.

"Where? How?"

"In the kitchen. On Christmas Eve. I'd come back downstairs to ask my mom if I could invite you to have Christmas dinner with us at my girlfriend's house. I didn't know you were still there. And I saw you kissing her."

He scratched at his jaw. "Josh. I—I'm sorry. We never meant to hurt you."

"Never mind about me," he replied, his voice suddenly protective. "What do you want from her?"

He stepped closer. "You don't think I know what you are? How many women you've dated and then dropped? And I admired you for it? How stupid of me."

Sam's mind was all jammed up. He hated being backed into a corner. Mariella had probably read the same articles. She knew about his past, but she cared for him anyway. He wasn't going to reveal his true feelings to anyone before he even had a chance to say the words to Mariella.

"Josh, you have the wrong idea about me. Don't believe everything you read."

"Do you really care about her?"

"I never meant to hurt your mother, and I never meant to hurt you."

Sam's eyes widened with alarm. The boy was near tears.

"I don't believe you. But if you really mean that, and if you're really not the liar I think you are, then stay out of our lives."

Sam watched as Josh grabbed his bag and ran off the field, choking back sobs. It occurred to him Mariella was probably in the parking lot, waiting to pick up her son. He debated running after him, and upon reaching her car, telling her all that had happened. Posing the question to her, right then and there.

Did she really want to never see him again?

But he turned away and continued tapping down clumps of grass, afraid of the answer.

Mariella reviewed the documents in her hands one last time, took a deep breath and then entered the mayor's office. She saw Gregory's trademark black fedora on his desk and a fresh flower arrangement, personally created by his wife, Vanessa.

"I have the report you'd asked for."

Gregory looked up. "Thanks for staying late to help me prepare for my meeting tomorrow."

She covered her nose and sneezed. "No problem. It was my pleasure."

There was concern in his hazel eyes. "Allergies?"

"No. Just a little cold."

Gregory shook his head, as he flipped through the pages. "I feel responsible. I know you've been working hard on this over the past several weeks."

"That's very kind, but this project was my idea."

"I hope you at least set it aside during your vacation."

She didn't want to think about the holiday because Sam was wrapped up in it.

"Let me take you through the document."

At the mayor's nod, she proceeded. "All the city projects you have in mind are listed, from the most expensive to the least. If there is a grant available that could be used to pay some or all of the costs, I've noted the name in the right-hand column."

Mariella waited patiently as he scanned the report. After a few minutes he got up and put his hat on, and then took his coat out of the closet.

"It appears to be time well spent. This is excellent work, Mariella. I'll give it a closer read tomorrow."

He slipped her report into his briefcase. "Whatever we can do to keep costs low and not raise taxes, we should do it. And this will give us a good start."

Mariella touched the collar of her navy turtleneck sweater and looked down briefly at her ivory pencil skirt.

"Mayor, I was wondering if I could set up some time to talk to you. It's about my job here."

His eyes narrowed. "You're doing wonderfully. What's the problem?"

She forced a smile. "As you know, I now have a degree in economics. I've enjoyed being your assistant, but I'm looking for something more."

"Understandable," he said. "Do you have a position in mind?"

"No. And that's the problem. I've been looking at the internal job listings and I don't see anything so far."

Gregory set his briefcase on the conference table. "What are you interested in doing?"

"I've found I really like grant writing, so I'm hoping to transition into a similar role."

"You're good at it, too. Congratulations on securing funding for another local playground."

She smiled. "Thank you. I'm now working on a grant application for artificial turf at the high school."

"I heard. No offense to Coach Lander, but Sam has really turned the team around."

And turned my world upside down.

Her relationship with Sam was over; she didn't want that to deter her from her goals. She had to focus on her future.

"Yes, Josh has really improved."

"All better from the injury?"

"He was a little wobbly in the beginning of the season, but he's done with physical therapy and scoring lots of goals. By the way, thanks for adding my idea to your list."

"Bay Point is a very walkable and rideable community. I want our residents to feel safe no matter how they choose to travel on our streets."

She nodded. "My research showed that dedicated bike lanes should help cut down on accidents. They're very popular now, so grants are competitive, but I think we have a good shot."

He adjusted his hat and walked out of his office. She followed him and closed the door.

"Though I'd hate to lose you to someone else, let me think about another role for you. I'll also check to see if there are job openings available that were not posted online."

"Thank you, Mayor," she said, exhaling with relief that she likely wouldn't have to move for a better job.

Mariella got her red peacoat and purse. It was after six o'clock at night, and she was late getting home.

They rode the elevator to the first floor of City Hall. Outside on the steps, Gregory turned to her.

"By the way, do you think Sam might consider staying in Bay Point?"

She tilted her head. "I'm not sure. Why?"

"I was thinking of starting a special recreation commission to help drive more participation in sports for boys and girls. I think he'd be a good leader for it, and I was hoping you could influence him to stay."

"I don't think I could," she replied.

He gave her a brief smile. "Really? I could have sworn I saw the two of you picnicking at Coquina Cove a couple of months ago."

"It wasn't me, Mayor," she said, with a firm shake of her head.

They said goodbye and Mariella walked over to Lucy's Bar and Grille. She picked up a couple of jerk chicken sandwiches, pasta salad and two sweet teas for dinner.

A part of her hoped she would run into Sam, but he wasn't there. She'd see him tomorrow at the vendor meeting for the artificial turf project.

As she drove past Relics and Rarities, she almost pulled around to the back to drop by his apartment. But what would she say when she got there?

Being in love was like being on high alert all the time. She didn't want to feel the constant butterflies in her stomach anymore, or feel her heart burst every time she heard someone say his name.

He knew that she loved him, but she would never say the words. Soccer season would be over in six weeks or so, and then he'd be back on a plane to the UK. And where did that leave her?

Same place she was now. Alone and hungry, and not for sandwiches.

She'd made a huge mistake in getting involved with Sam. Instead of putting aside her desires, like she had for years, she'd allowed Sam to flatter and pursue her.

His sexy body, his British accent and his out-of-this-world lovemaking skills were the kryptonite that doomed her. The reins on her heart had been broken and thrown aside. She'd gone galloping after him into the sunset, but had somehow missed the happy ending.

Mariella pulled into her driveway and by habit, steeled herself for an argument. Josh had been pretty quiet over the past two weeks and she was starting to worry.

When she walked through the back door, she raised a brow, surprised to see him doing his homework at the kitchen table. Since freshman year, he'd always done his homework up in his room.

"Hey, I've got your favorite."

She set the bag of food down on the counter and noticed he was still in his uniform.

They had a rule where he was supposed to change as soon as he got home. Then he was to put his grass- and mud-stained uniform to presoak in the washing machine.

But by the strained look on his face, she decided that now wasn't the time to remind him.

"How was practice today?"

"It was okay. Coach and I talked."

She feigned indifference. "Oh? About what?"

"You."

"Me? Why?" she asked without turning around.

"I told him I saw you kissing him on Christmas Eve."

The pit in her stomach deepened. She didn't need to ask how. It was enough that he saw.

"I asked him if he cared about you."

Mariella slowly faced him. "What did he say?"

"He wouldn't respond. And then I told him to stay away from you."

She frowned and her heart sank. "You shouldn't have done that, Josh. It's really none of your business."

"Why? He doesn't want you," he yelled. "Haven't you read any of the blogs and articles about him?"

"I have, but sometimes people can change."

Josh shook his head stubbornly. "Not someone like him. All he cares about is winning and keeping his player image. He doesn't care about you."

She flinched at his mean tone and said, "You're going off to college soon. You'll have your own life. And I need mine."

There was a long pause and she thought the conversation was over.

"Are you in love with him?"

Josh immediately looked embarrassed, and Mariella knew it was a hard question for him to ask.

He slumped back in his chair. "I care about you, Mom. I want you to be happy, but it won't happen with him."

"No comment. Besides, it doesn't matter, Josh. There's nothing going on between us."

"What about if I quit the team? Then you wouldn't have to see him again," he offered.

"No! You'll see the season through to the end. And so will I. End of discussion."

She unwrapped the sandwiches and set the sweet teas on the table. "Now, let's eat. Before the food gets cold."

Chapter 13

Sam woke with a start. Something was vibrating against his head. He leaned up on one elbow, shoved his hand under his pillow and brought out his phone. The glow of the screen was a shock to his eyes as was the time.

It was well after midnight. The tent between his legs slowly subsided, and he knew he must have been dreaming about Mariella.

He collapsed against the pillow and put the phone to his ear.

"This better be good, Niles."

"You're making the milk in my coffee turn sour. Don't sound so glum, mate."

He shut his eyes to ward off the grogginess and his annoyance. "I'm not glum, I'm exhausted, and you've interrupted what would have been a very nice dream."

"It's early here, too. Talk nice, I've got you on speakerphone."

The voice on the other end was a little too cheerful.

"Why are you so chipper at this hour in the morning?"

Sam heard the loud purr of Niles's Siamese cat, Angie, and he felt himself start to relax at the sound.

"Because I'm about to change your whole life."

His ears perked up even more. Right now he could use a bit of good news.

"Oh yeah, how?"

"I've just brokered a deal to make you the new head coach of the Emeralds. Since you're not sure you want to play soccer again, this will give you some time to think it over."

"What happened to the current coach?"

"Have you been hiding under a rock?"

Sam slid a hand behind his head and tried to get comfortable again. "I've been trying to, but you keep on finding me."

Niles snorted, and Sam knew he was not amused.

"The man was jailed three weeks ago on suspicion of supplying performance-enhancing drugs to his team members."

"Hmm...so that's why they've been winning matches."

"Well, they're losing now," he said, gleefully. "Half the team has been suspended."

Sam sat up against the headboard, leaned over and turned on the lamp. No way he could go to sleep now.

"Okay. Talk to me."

"You'll have the opportunity to recruit players. Be your own boss. Best of all, little chance for injury."

"Travel would be the same, right?"

"Sure, but you always liked that. More places to go, more women to meet."

"More scandals for you to hash up," Sam interrupted.

Niles laughed. "No need for those when you're a coach. In fact, you want your image to stay as boring as possible."

"Actually, I was thinking of staying in Bay Point."

"Why?"

Yesterday Brian told him Coach Lander had decided to retire. If he wanted the head coach position permanently, it was his for the taking, but he wasn't ready to share the details with his agent.

"I don't know. Sun always shines, rarely any rain."

"Is it the weather or that woman?"

That woman.

Sam chuckled. "You always were a shrewd man."

"And I've got the perfect solution. Just bring her along for the ride."

"It's more serious than that, Niles. I love her."

Niles grunted. "Wow. That's the first time I've heard you say you love anything other than soccer."

"Anyway," Sam continued. "I don't think it will work, dragging her with me. She's a package deal. She's got a teenage kid who will be going to college in September."

"Ever hear of a gap year? Bring him along, too. I'm sure he'd love to travel Europe on your dime."

Sam shook his head. "All I can say is I'll think about it."

"That's all I can ask of you at one o'clock in the morning. You talk to your girl. In the meantime, I'll continue to hammer out the details."

"All right, say good-night, Niles."

"Make me proud, Sam."

"So I can make you more money, right?"

"Isn't that what life is all about?"

Sam hung up. He wasn't sure what life was about, but his definitely had less meaning without Mariella in it.

Later that same day

Mariella crossed her legs at her ankles, settling back on a park bench to wait, holding a tissue to her nose. She hugged her arms against her red peacoat, trying to stay warm and ease her anxiety.

After the vendor meeting yesterday, she had asked Leslie to meet her at the town square. She was tired of not knowing what the woman would do with the damning information she had about her and Sam.

Leslie was not someone she considered a friend, but she was a fellow advocate for the kids of Bay Point High. She was hoping to appeal to her kinder, gentler nature, if she even had one, to let it go. Maybe she already had, but Mariella needed confirmation.

She sneezed and smoothed imaginary wrinkles from her beige pants. Over the past several days, her cold had gotten worse.

Though she didn't know it, Leslie was holding her back from truly getting over Sam. In a way, she had not only caused the distance between them, she was also standing in the way of closing it.

Heels tapped on the pavement and she looked up and raised a brow as Leslie approached, carrying two paper cups. She didn't automatically assume the beverage was for her, since Leslie's husband's office was close by.

She rubbed the tissue against her nose. "Ah-choo!"

"Bless you," Leslie said, handing her one. "Herbal green tea with lemon and honey. You sounded as if you could have used this yesterday."

Mariella took it from her, touched at the gesture, but also wary of it.

"You noticed, huh?"

"I think everyone in the meeting did."

She balled up the tissue and stuck it in her purse.

"Thank you. This is very kind." Her voice had a croaking sound to it, to match her raspy throat.

"I need it more today, but at least I haven't started coughing yet."

She pried off the plastic lid and took a tentative sip of the hot drink, wondering how to begin what could be a difficult conversation.

"I guess I've been worrying myself sick."

Leslie, dressed in black skinny jeans and a white turtleneck sweater, sat down.

"Over what?" she asked, turning toward her.

As if you didn't know, Mariella thought.

She reached into her purse and pulled out a folded piece of paper. "This."

Leslie met her eyes, took it from her and read it quickly. "It's a resignation letter. You're stepping down from your post as PTA vice president?"

"I thought it would be the best thing, before you kicked me out anyway."

Mariella had thought long and hard about the decision, having devoted so much time to the organization. When Josh was a freshman, she was simply a member of the PTA, but in subsequent years she rose through the ranks, serving as secretary, treasurer and finally, vice president.

Leslie folded the paper and laid it aside. "I can't deny I've thought about it. Sam is incredibly hot, but what you guys did and where you did it was incredibly stupid. You're actually lucky I was the one who discovered you."

"I know and I can promise you it will never happen again."

Leslie nudged her in the side with her elbow.

"At least on school grounds, right?"

"Maybe never again, anywhere. I broke it off with him."

She raised a brow. "You did what?"

"I broke up with him."

"Because of me?"

Mariella thought she saw a little smile cross Leslie's mouth, which put her on guard once again.

She debated telling her Josh had caught them, too. Her son no longer trusted Sam had her best interests in mind, and she was inclined to agree with him. Sam was just a sexual thrill-seeker, and she was just along for the ride.

"I admit I was very concerned about what you'd do. That night you hinted there would be consequences, but you left it open as to what they would be."

"I was shocked, Mariella. I mean, wouldn't you be, if the roles were reversed?" Leslie curled a finger on her chin. "Come to think of it, I wouldn't mind being in Sam's arms."

Mariella looked at her sideways. "You're married, remember?"

She grinned innocently. "A woman can still fantasize, can't she?"

"Of course, just not about my man."

Leslie laughed, and then her expression turned solemn, and her voice quieted. "In some respects, I'm jealous of you, Mariella."

Her eyes widened. "Jealous of me? Why? You have a wonderful husband who loves and adores you."

"Ha!" Leslie snorted. "Loves, yes. Adores? Not so much. I wish he would look at me the way Sam looked at you."

"You're wrong about Sam." She covered her nose with a clean tissue and sneezed.

"Maybe you couldn't tell, but I could."

Mariella shrugged her shoulders. "He was sitting in the back of the room. I was at the front."

"Right. And I was sitting next to him. I could tell he was having a hard time maintaining his focus on the vendor presentations. His eyes kept on floating over to you."

"And I was doing my best to ignore him."

Leslie pointed a finger at her and laughed. "See, you did notice."

"Did anyone else see, too?" she asked with a tentative smile.

It felt like she and Leslie were two teenagers discussing a crush.

"No. Principal Taylor and Brian didn't have a clue. They were too busy waiting for the cost portion of the Power-Point decks."

"Do you think there are some people in town who know about us?"

"Not sure. Maybe. Are you surprised?"

Mariella nodded her head. "Yes, I am, actually."

"I may like to talk about people, but I'm not evil."

"Then why do it?"

Leslie looked her straight in the eye. "Because I'm nosy, and because I like comparing other people's lives to my own. Isn't that awful?"

When Mariella did not reply, Leslie continued. "Can I give you some advice?"

She nodded, and mentally braced herself.

"If he's in love with you, don't let that go. If you do, you'll never know where it leads."

Mariella held the tea in both hands. "You're not going to tell anyone, are you?"

Leslie shook her head. "No, but only because I remember how it used to be with my husband and me. How we couldn't keep our hands to ourselves. I took that time for granted, and now I'm paying for it."

She felt like hugging Leslie, but didn't want to make her uncomfortable.

"Thanks. I'd better get to work."

Both women stood, and Mariella's resignation letter

slipped to the ground. Leslie picked it up, tore it in half and handed the pieces to her.

"Here. I can't accept this. You helped the PTA raise more money in the three years you've been involved than anybody else. Nobody stretches a dollar like you do."

Mariella stared at her. "Are you sure?"

"Yeah. Think of it as a belated Christmas gift. Now get out of here before I change my mind."

This time Mariella did hug her, and Leslie hugged her back.

Sam pushed through the revolving door of City Hall, and entered the rotunda. There was a small cart set up inside that sold sandwiches and beverages, and a line had already formed.

The elderly security guard manning the desk near a bank of elevators appeared to be half-asleep.

"Excuse me."

Sam pressed the small dome-shaped bell. The man roused to attention.

"I'm sorry, I didn't mean to startle you."

"At my age, sometimes I need a jump start to the heart. This little bell helps. What can I do for you?"

Sam saw the man's name badge: Prentice.

"I'm looking for the mayor's office."

Rather than wait for Mariella to approach him, he was going to talk to her.

She can't ignore me here.

He had to know if she loved him, and then he could figure everything else out later.

Following his conversation with Niles, he wasn't able to go back to sleep. He'd lain in bed, thinking of what he should do. Stay in Bay Point or take the coaching position back home in England?

There were pros and cons to both.

Here in Bay Point, he could live in relative anonymity. In time, his star status would dwindle and he'd be considered a permanent resident of the community. Maybe someday, he might even apply to become a United States citizen.

He could also focus on the game he loved, and continue the work of building the Titan soccer team into the powerhouse he knew it could be.

But what about the woman he loved? If she didn't feel the same way, he wasn't sure he'd be able to live here, knowing he wasn't the one for her. His pride would be hurt, but even worse, he wasn't too confident his heart would recover as quickly as he would need it to.

A gnarled finger pointed at him. "Sign the book."

Sam scrawled his name. Prentice noted the day and time, and gave him a wide-eyed look.

"Hey, I've heard about you. You're the guy who's putting Bay Point soccer on the map."

"Thanks, but the kids do all the work," he said, refusing to take all the credit.

With his thumb, Prentice pushed the brim of his cap farther up on his head. It was khaki-green, which, other than the white shirt, was the same color as the rest of his uniform.

"I've been to a few games. I wish my legs and feet could move as fast as theirs, then maybe Miss Maisie wouldn't be able to catch me."

Sam smiled. "Now if you could direct me to the mayor's office?"

"Oh, yeah." The guard scratched his head. "Elevators behind me to the second floor. Then go down the hall and to the right."

A thought occurred to him. "Is Mariella back from lunch?"

"Yes," Prentice said, nodding. "But come to think of it, the mayor just left twenty minutes ago. You may want to come back later."

"Thanks for the tip, but I think Mariella will be able to help me with what I need."

Prentice shrugged. "Suit yourself."

Sam stopped at the food cart and afterward, went to the elevator. Exiting on the second floor, his sneakers screeched on the polished tile.

He rounded the corner and saw Mariella emerging from an office he assumed was the mayor's.

She closed the door, and he heard her sharp intake of breath. "Sam, what are you doing here?"

There was a sandwich on her desk, unwrapped, and also a big bouquet of flowers. He assumed the sandwich came from the cart downstairs, but who had given her the flowers?

"Mariella, I hate to bother you on your lunch hour, but I had to see you. Is there someplace we can talk privately?"

Her expression was wary. "Sure, we can go into the conference room. What's in the bag?"

"Chicken soup. In the vendor meeting, I noticed you weren't feeling well." He gave her a slow grin. "Plus, you've been pretty cold to me for the past couple of weeks. Since you wouldn't let me see you, I had to do something to warm you up."

"Ha-ha. Lower your voice."

"But there's no one around."

"That's what we thought the first time." She held a tissue to her nose and took the paper sack. "Thanks. I'm feeling better now."

"Because of me, or because of those flowers on your desk?" he asked, encouraged by the hint of a smile on her lips.

"Maybe a little bit of both. Follow me. The conference room is right down the hall."

When they entered the room, he asked her to close the door. "What I need to tell you is private." She hesitated and he said, "I won't bite, though I know you like it."

Mariella gave him an exasperated look and shut the door. He slid out of his black jacket and settled into a chair. It took his entire strength not to grab her by the arm and pull her onto his lap.

"It's quiet here. Is that normal?"

"No. The mayor and a few of his aides left for a meeting a little while ago. There's some vacant land that belongs to the city in the southeast corner of Bay Point where he is considering building affordable townhomes."

"Hmm…keep me posted. I may or may not be in the market for one."

She did not sit down, and leaned against the table next to him. "So you're considering staying in Bay Point?"

"That depends on a lot of things."

She tilted her head and seemed to consider his statement, but didn't press him further. "Actually, I'm glad you stopped by."

At her words, hope of a reconciliation raced through him. He touched her hand and kept his voice light. "You've missed me as much as I've missed you. Is that it?"

Sam was relieved when she nodded. "I have missed you. A lot. But that doesn't change the facts."

"Which are?"

She took a deep breath. "Josh knows about us."

"Yes. He told me to stay away from you."

"And I told him I would," she replied. "I can't break a promise to my son."

Sam got up, cupped his hand behind her neck and brought her face to his.

"Then how about I break it for you?" he whispered. "I still want to be with you."

She pushed him away. "It's not that simple, Sam. I don't want Josh to get hurt. I dated a few men when he was younger and he got emotionally attached to one or two. When things didn't work out, he was devastated because the men weren't sincere."

She turned her back on him, and his heart sank as she walked over to the office window.

"There is no you and me anymore."

"It doesn't have to be that way, Mariella."

Her words had squelched his courage and now he wasn't sure if he was ready to tell her he loved her. Not until he found out where he stood.

He went to where she sat on the windowsill, and sat next to her.

"It's Leslie, isn't it? You're still worried about what she might do."

"She's not going to tell. She's going to keep what she saw under wraps. I arranged to meet with her this morning, before work. I was afraid she wasn't going to show up, but she did."

"What did she say?"

Mariella seemed to consider her next words. "She understood why it had happened."

Sam folded his arms in disbelief. "She empathized with us? And what was her reasoning?"

"Past experience, I gather, but she didn't offer any specifics."

"That's good, right? Good for us?"

"It is good, but good for us? I'm not sure."

He touched her arm. "I'm thinking about going back to England, once the season is over."

"I understand and I hope you make a decision soon.

Quite frankly, I'm tired of your flip-flopping. One minute you want to stay in Bay Point, the next minute you don't. I don't want to start anything again we can't finish."

"Just calm down and listen to me, okay? My agent is negotiating a deal for me, where I would coach another team instead of play professionally. I want you to come back home with me."

Her eyes widened. "And leave Josh?"

"He can take a gap year and come with us. Or there are plenty of wonderful universities in the United Kingdom."

"When would you have to start?"

"Right after the season ends."

She bit her lip. "I don't think I'm ready to move, let alone take our relationship to the next step. Don't hinge your decision on me."

"I'm not, but you're important to me. Too important to leave without taking a chance to ask if you'll go with me."

"Do what is in your heart."

He took her hands in his, brought them to his lips.

"You're in my heart."

Her eyes filled with tears. "I can't go with you, Sam."

"But I thought you were bored with your job. You said you were looking for something new and challenging. If you didn't find it, you would leave."

She slipped away and sat down at the table.

"Right, but I spoke with the mayor. He's looking to see if there's anything available."

Sam stood and leaned against the wall with a tight smile. "That's wonderful."

"But not necessarily for us," Mariella said, and he noticed the sad tone in her voice.

"Everywhere we turn there seems to be a brick wall."

He joined her at the table, just to be near her.

"There must be some way for us to break through, and I'm not going to stop until I find it."

Mariella turned to him. "Why is this so important to you?"

"Don't you know?"

She shook her head and he touched his lips to hers, his heart about to burst with emotion.

"You and I have a future together."

"I'm sorry, Sam. My future is here. I'm not leaving Bay Point."

He frowned and was about to continue to try to change her mind when his phone rang. He dug it out of his pocket, saw who it was, and his stomach clenched.

"Excuse me," he said, turning slightly in his seat.

"Where are you?" he said, keeping his eye on Mariella, who didn't look happy at the interruption.

He listened again and stood. "I'll be there as soon as I can."

"Who was it?" she asked, dabbing at her eyes with a tissue as he zipped up his jacket.

He slipped his phone into his pocket. "My mother. She's in town and wants me to pick her up at the airport."

Chapter 14

His mother, Ida Kelly, was a year short of sixty, but could pass for forty. She kept her body trim with daily walks around their neighborhood, and occasional visits from her personal trainer. Her skin was smooth, wrinkle-free and untarnished, like a newly minted copper penny, which was apropos because she cherished money. And had plenty of it.

Sam's father was a prosperous banker and had been adored by local townspeople for his willingness to lend his financial advice, especially if they hadn't qualified for a loan. He had done well for himself and his family over the years, and when he passed away, he'd made good on his promise to take care of his wife forever.

Ida had never worked, and would never have to as long as she lived. Sam thought she had too much time on her hands. Maybe if she had a real job, she wouldn't butt into his personal life.

He brought in the last of his mother's suitcases and put them at the base of the stairwell.

"Mariella, I really appreciate you letting Ida stay in your home. As you know, my place is too small."

She raised a brow as she counted the luggage. "Only nine? Are you sure she's only visiting and not moving in?"

"Knowing my mother, it's anyone's guess. But I'm praying it's just a visit."

And a short one, he thought, *for both of our sakes.*

Ida claimed she'd decided on the spur of the moment to take a two-week mini vacation in the States. He hoped her travels included another destination besides Bay Point.

His mother was mum on her plans, and when Ida wanted to keep a secret, no one could coax it out of her.

A piece of gossip, however? All she needed was a willing ear.

"I'm sorry I couldn't convince her to stay at the Horizon, and Maisie's was booked."

"She wants to treat my home like a bed-and-breakfast. She offered me money for her stay."

"Take it," he advised her. "If you refuse, you'll never hear the end of it, and nor will I."

He suspected the only reason his mother left her beloved country was to convince him to come back with her. But it was one of those situations where if he asked her, it would start a conversation—or an argument—that he didn't want to have, so it was better to stay quiet.

"It's no problem. The guest room is available and I'm happy to help as long as I can."

He understood Mariella's reluctance to commit to a time frame. She had a busy life with her son. The last game of the regular season was tomorrow and the playoffs would begin. And after that, who knew where life would lead either of them?

Sam wiped his hands on his navy blue athletic pants.

"Do you want me to bring the bags up to her room? It's right next to your room, right?"

He had an ulterior motive besides helping his mother. He had never seen Mariella's bedroom, and probably never would, so was hoping to get a peek inside. He wanted to feel close to her, and getting a look at where she laid her head down at night and got dressed in the morning would help.

"No, while you were outside and I showed her to her room, she told me to not disturb her. Don't worry about her suitcases. Josh will get those when he gets home."

Sam shrugged his shoulders. "Okay. I guess tell her to call me when she gets up."

He followed Mariella to the back door, noting the graceful sway in her walk. Was she purposefully trying to entice him when she knew he couldn't do anything about it?

"Sam? I hope you don't mind me asking, but why is she here? You never mentioned she'd be visiting."

"Because I didn't know. But if I had to guess she's here to check out where I've been living for the past few months and who I've been hanging out with."

Mariella got quiet. "We were doing a lot more than hanging out."

Sam took her hand in his. "I miss those times very much."

"I do, too," she admitted. "But they brought us more trouble than we needed. Now that it's over, both of our lives will be calmer now."

He opened the door, turned and kissed her on the top of her forehead.

"You mean boring and unexciting, right?"

"I mean calm," she replied firmly. "Let's just keep it that way, okay?"

Mariella gave him a playful shove and shut the door.

"Keep dreaming, babe," Sam muttered under his breath as he pulled out of the driveway.

He knew he would never stop dreaming about her.

Mariella stood by the oven and glanced over at the woman who had stayed with her for the past two weeks. She felt as though she was being watched and evaluated on everything. From her housekeeping and cooking skills to the way she raised her son.

Not outwardly, or in any way that would be obvious to anyone but her. Ida had been nothing but polite, sometimes overly so, but expected to be waited on hand and foot.

"More tea, Mrs. Kelly? I can boil some more hot water, if you'd like."

Ida shook her head. "Even though your tea-making skills have improved since I got here, I must decline."

Mariella frowned inwardly. Ida had a way of saying no that made her feel guilty. She rinsed the breakfast dishes and placed them in the dishwasher. Josh had already left for school and she had to get to work.

Today she had a couple of interviews at City Hall so she was wearing her gray pantsuit. She purchased a new white silk tank to go under it and added a small string of pearls.

Ida eased her thin frame out of her chair and placed the teacup and saucer on the counter. Dressed in taupe wool pants, an ivory blouse and a red cardigan sweater, Ida appeared comfortable and elegant.

"Henry is picking me up soon. We're going to San Francisco for the day."

She gave her a sideways smile. "How nice. Another buying trip?"

Sam's mother had purchased a number of antiques during her stay, some of which were stored in her garage, leaving little room for her own car.

Ida laughed, unaware at the offhanded dig, or maybe she just didn't care, Mariella surmised.

"No, just sightseeing today. But you never know, the best finds are the unexpected ones."

"True," she replied as she put the orange juice back into the refrigerator.

But she wasn't talking about antiques.

Meeting Sam had been completely unexpected. She hadn't known he would walk into the gift shop, and she certainly hadn't expected to fall in love with him.

"Will you be back in time for dinner?"

"Doubtful," Ida said.

Mariella frowned. Sam had been eating dinner with them every night, so she had gotten used to spending time with him, even if it was only as a friend.

At first, it was difficult as she was so used to cooking for just her and Josh. But as the days went on, she got better at it. It helped that Sam and his mother were appreciative and noticed her efforts.

Sometimes Sam picked up Ida and took her to breakfast. On those occasions, she was lucky enough to see him twice.

But most days, he would arrive with Josh after soccer practice, and soon after they would all have dinner together. It was almost like they were a family. She would miss that feeling when Ida went home, and Sam had no reason to come around.

Only because I won't let him, she said to herself, knowing the reason she was keeping her distance was because she wanted to lessen the pain she would feel once he was gone for good.

"Josh forgot his jacket again," Ida commented, pointing to where it was slung over a kitchen chair.

Like her, Josh initially wasn't pleased with their sudden guest. It had just been the two of them in the house for years, so having to share it with someone else was difficult for the both of them.

Oddly, Ida had grown on the boy, and they seemed to enjoy each other's company. She was teaching him how to play chess and he liked to ask her questions about her travels throughout Europe and Asia. He seemed enthralled with her stories.

She hung the forgotten garment on the coatrack in the mudroom. "Don't worry, Ida. He always keeps a second one in his locker."

"Has he decided on what college he will attend?"

Mariella shook her head. "Since he decided against early decision, we won't hear until March which ones have accepted him." She sighed heavily. "It's going to be so hard to let him go."

Ida leaned against the counter. "I know, but you will. That's what mums like us have to do. I remember the day when I dropped Sam off at university. I cried all the way home, and the next day, too. But then I realized that in order for Sam to grow into a man, he had to fill his own larder and flap his own wings."

"Was he always as independent as he is now?"

"Yes, after my husband died, he had to be. I know he felt an obligation to take care of me, as any good son would, but I do hope he knows I'd never want to be a burden to him."

Mariella raised a brow, surprised she had something in common with Ida.

"Sometimes I'm afraid Josh will feel the same way."

She filled her travel mug with coffee. "Maybe that's why you and he get along so well. You understand him in a way most adults would not."

Ida nodded, watching her. "I've learned how to let go. Something I think you may need to get better at."

"What do you mean?" she asked, not believing Ida one bit. If she had no problem letting go of her son, then why was she here watching his every move?

"I see the way you look at Sam when he is here for dinner. And I see the way Sam looks at you. You're both crazy about each other. The question is what are you going to do about it?"

Was this a trick? Mariella thought, looping her purse over her shoulder. She hoped Ida would take the hint. If she didn't leave soon, she would be late for work.

"Sam and I have agreed that pursuing a relationship would not be in the best interest of either of us."

Ida *tsk-tsked.* "I know you don't want my opinion, but I think you're both being naive."

Mariella nearly dropped her coffee, not expecting that kind of remark. "You do? Why?"

"I admit, when I first arrived I was extremely skeptical of you. I thought you would detract from his career. Plus, I didn't want Sam to be involved with someone who already had a teenage son."

"Just because I'm over thirty doesn't mean I can't have any more children, Ida," she huffed. "Women are waiting longer and longer to have kids these days."

"I know, and I realize now how selfish I was being. Josh is a wonderful young man. You've done a great job with him," Ida added.

"And what about Sam?" Mariella asked, curious now about her opinion.

"I know my son. Sam is obviously very fond of you, and if you're both smart, you won't ruin a chance for love that you both might not ever find again."

Mariella jangled her keys in her hand. "It sounds like you've just given your blessing. I appreciate it, but unfortunately, this is not your decision to make."

She sighed heavily. "I know, but a mother should have some say in who her son should be with, and I'm just saying I hope Sam chooses you."

Mariella smiled and hugged her. "Does your son know you're trying to be a matchmaker?"

Ida put her finger to her lips. "Let's just keep it our little secret."

Sam pressed Mariella's front doorbell and waited, flowers in hand. With a grimace he realized that given what he'd learned in the past few hours, he wasn't sure if there was anything to celebrate. Still, he'd gone home and put on a clean, white shirt and blue jeans, no tie, rather than stay in his coaching outfit, so he'd look his best for her.

If Mariella was home, he knew she would be alone. Last night at dinner, he'd overheard Josh reminding her he would be at a friend's house today. His mother was off on another buying trip with Henry Wexler.

She opened the door, her face beaming. It was going to be hard to pretend he didn't know the reason why.

"Hi, beautiful. These are for you."

He handed her a beautiful bouquet of deep pink tulips and yellow daffodils, and then gathered her into his arms.

She lowered her nose into the flowers. "Hmm…smells like spring. What's the special occasion?"

Her hair was tied up, and she was casually dressed in a white T-shirt with a gold sunflower on it and mustard-colored jeans.

"Time alone with you," he said, kissing her tenderly.

It had been beyond wonderful to be able to spend every night with her over the past two weeks. Even though she wasn't in his bed at the time, at least she was in his presence. He'd been able to look at her, talk with her, over her delicious meals. It felt like they were a real couple, and he liked it.

"That is always something to celebrate," she murmured against his lips. "I've missed you."

"I'm here now," he said, but his last word hung in the air, like the last apple on a tree.

Mariella nudged him away with her shoulder, pulled him inside and shut the door.

"You'll never believe what happened."

"Try me," he said, playing along.

He took the flowers, and got what Mariella called her "everyday" vase, from the cupboard underneath the kitchen sink. She used the modest plastic as a holding vessel until she had time to transfer and arrange the stems into one of the other vases she had scattered throughout her house.

"I ran into Maisie Barnell, and she told me your mother actually paid her for a room, but declined to sleep in it. She's had a room available this entire time."

This was news to him, and he was appalled. He shook his head. "And I believed her when she told me the B & B was full. I'm sorry, Mariella."

He finished filling the vase with water, and she began to drop the stems into it.

"Don't be. I admit, I was mad at first. I felt like I'd been duped. But she and Josh are getting along so well, I don't feel it's necessary to mention I know."

Sam wiped his hands on a towel. "That's why I—"

He stopped short of saying the word *love*, even though he knew deep down that was what he felt. But his feelings didn't matter now.

"That's why I admire you," he finished. "You have the ability to overlook the imposition of others. My mother did a very dishonest thing."

"We both know she just wanted to learn more about me, and what better way than to board in my home?"

He stayed quiet until she had put the last stem in the vase. "At least one thing good came out of it. We got to be together more."

"Yeah, under your mother's watchful eye."

His heart clenched and they shared a brief embrace.

"I also have some good news," Mariella continued, motioning to him to follow her into the living room.

He chanced draping his arm around her on the couch, grateful when she let it remain on her shoulders, and snuggled closer.

"As you know, I've been interviewing, but haven't had much luck. Gregory hinted yesterday that he was going to create a new role just for me. It will be centered around grant writing, as well as managing any new citywide project initiatives."

Sam leaned his head back, not sure if he should ruin the moment, but the words slipped out before he could cinch them in.

"I know. I heard."

She turned and braced her left shoulder against the sofa. "You did? How?"

"Gregory was at the flower shop when I picked up the bouquet I had ordered from Vanessa. He told me about his conversation with you, and asked me to convince you to take the job."

Her tone sounded confused. "I never told him or anyone else about our relationship. I wonder why he felt he had to tell you?"

Sam patted her knee, knowing how much she valued her privacy. "Don't blame the mayor. It was my fault. He asked me who the flowers were for, and I told him they were for you. Maybe he thought you told me at soccer practice. I'm sorry."

"That makes sense. He knows I'm working on the artificial turf project and that you've been involved in some of the meetings."

She gave him a tentative smile, but he could tell she was eager to hear more of their conversation.

"Did he say anything else?"

He nodded. "You're the hardest worker he's ever known, the most qualified and you've had more input on the revitalization of Bay Point than most people knew."

Mariella dropped her chin, and he saw liquid swimming in her eyes.

"Hey," he said, lifting her chin with the tip of one finger. "I thought this would make you happy. Why the tears?"

She swiped at her eyes with the back of her hand. "It just feels so nice to be recognized. Even though there were some aspects of my job I really didn't like, I always gave one hundred percent."

"I told the mayor I would use all my persuasive powers to convince you to take the position."

He planted a trail of kisses down her neck behind her ear, enjoying her scent. "How am I doing so far?"

"I already decided I would take it, Sam."

She giggled, pushing him away again. "Before you started kissing me."

He wanted to laugh, but he couldn't.

"Gregory also let me know he got approval from city council to create a recreation board and he wants me to lead it."

He saw hope flare in her eyes. "And what did you say?"

"I turned him down."

"Why, Sam?"

"I've faced the fact that I'll never play professional soccer again, not because I can't, but I do need a change. I accepted the coaching job in England."

He took her hands in his and stared into her eyes, but the light he saw in them before was gone, and all that remained was pain.

"The contract is signed, Mariella."

She frowned, slipping her hands away. "But I thought you were thinking about staying here. You've said as much many times over dinner. Or was that just a ploy to keep your mother, and me, on our toes?"

He shook his head. "I actually spoke to my agent a day or two after our conversation in the conference room. When you told me you were dead-set against moving to England and that you were tired of my indecision."

Her hurt tone wrenched at his heart, but the accusation behind it angered him a little. They'd spent time together, not enough for either of them, but he thought she knew him better than to insinuate his words were less than genuine.

"I don't play games, Mariella. It's true I was thinking about staying in Bay Point permanently. But like you, I would be making a mistake if I didn't pursue this chance. We each have a great career opportunity in front of us."

She slumped against the couch, clearly upset. "You and Josh have gotten much closer over the past several weeks. He's going to be so disappointed you're not staying in Bay Point."

He sat up and put his elbows on his knees. "This isn't about Josh, Mariella. It's about you. What are you feeling right now?"

"Me? I care about you, Sam. But I was always ready to say goodbye."

He turned toward her, ready to protest, but the strength behind her words had taken his resolve away.

She took a deep breath. "Every time I talk to my own

mom, I don't complain how hard it is to be a single mother, but somehow she hears it in my voice. She asks me 'when are you going to put yourself first?'"

Mariella leaned forward and put her hands over his.

"I've been putting myself dead last for years. Now this is my chance to start a new chapter in my life. Can you understand that?"

No matter how hard he tried, Sam knew it would be difficult to get her to change her mind. Though he felt Mariella belonged with him in England, it was clear she wanted to stay in Bay Point.

"It's my chance, too, Mariella."

She nodded, and he didn't wipe away the tears falling down her cheeks.

He stood, and wished he could get rid of the entire painful conversation. "Since we've both made up our minds, I guess there's nothing else to say, is there?"

Without another word, Sam walked out, regretting he opened up his heart to Mariella in the first place.

Chapter 15

Sam watched his mother as she moved about his apartment. She was returning to Great Britain, and though he loved her, he couldn't wait until he could resume some semblance of normalcy.

If normal is even possible, he thought. Without Mariella, his life would be emptier than it ever was before.

"A man with your money and credentials shouldn't be living in such a tiny hovel. I bet you can't wait to get back to your flat at home."

"Don't worry, Mum. Niles is taking care of everything."

He rubbed his eyes and then drank some water, tired of feeling so sluggish all the time. Losing Mariella was taking a toll, but he had to keep it together for his team, who would soon play the biggest game of the season.

"He better," Ida warned, shaking a finger. "Or he'll have me to answer to."

"I wouldn't wish that on anyone," Sam said, forcing a laugh.

"I won't get a chance to say a final goodbye to Josh and Mariella, so will you give them both my regards tomorrow?"

"Of course, and I'm sorry you won't be here to see the Titans in the first game of the playoffs."

"Me, too, but London is calling. Did you remember to have my bags and other items shipped yesterday?"

Sam grinned. At least with his mother, he always knew where he stood. "Yes, and it cost me a fortune."

"Better than dealing with it at the airport."

She patted his cheek like she used to do when he was a kid. "Don't look so sad. I will tell you the same thing I told her. It's clear you two belong together."

He wondered why Mariella didn't mention their woman-to-woman conversation. Another sign she was completely done with him and their relationship.

"A little too late. She's staying here. The mayor is going to give her the job she always wanted."

"If she doesn't have the man she always wanted," Ida said, "it's not going to be the same."

"Try telling her."

"I think I'll leave that up to you."

She zipped up her black leisure jacket, topped over a pair of tailored black wool pants, both of which she deemed her traveling clothes. "Lord, it's chilly in here, but I'm glad I got a chance to visit with you before I catch my flight."

He gave her a curious look, wondering why she seemed so happy. "Is that the only reason?"

"Perhaps." She giggled, eyes flashing. "By the way, you really got home late yesterday."

"I went to the bar and watched soccer till three a.m. How did you know?" Sam asked, suddenly suspicious.

"We heard you coming up the stairs around that time."

"We heard me?" he repeated.

"Yes, Mr. Wexler and I."

Now he'd heard everything. "Explain."

"Well, we were arguing about the antiquarian merits of the Staffordshire cat versus the Staffordshire dog, and one thing led to another and—"

He held up his hand and she giggled again. "I don't need the details, but I'm happy for you, Mum." He checked his watch. "We better get going. I don't want you to miss your flight."

They went downstairs and Sam paused by the back door of the antiques store.

"What about your boyfriend?" he asked with a wry smile.

"Henry will be in London in a few weeks, so I don't need to say goodbye, and neither do you."

Sam gave her a placating smile, but he was no fool.

Whatever he and Mariella had was over. There would be no more good luck kisses, no more sex on the beach and no more chances to show his love for her.

Sometimes a goodbye was meant to be forever.

"Josh, hurry up. We don't want to be late."

Tonight was the first playoff game of the post-season, and the Titans were favored to win. It was a home game, so they didn't have to travel, but she wanted to get there early so she could see Sam before the game started.

After today she would never see him again, unless she turned on the television.

Ida had returned to England yesterday. The house was quiet again, at least when she didn't have to yell for her son.

Mariella stood at the base of the stairs, waiting for Josh to emerge from his room, and had a flashback. Not long ago there was a chance Josh would never play soccer again, but he'd made a complete recovery. Sam had played a part by encouraging his love for the game and patiently coaching him through the trouble spots.

She slumped against the wall not knowing what she would say when she saw Sam tonight. She couldn't let him leave Bay Point being hurt or angry with her. It was important to convince him that the time they'd spent together had meant something to her. He had changed her life in a good way.

Josh bounded down the stairs. She never mentioned her conversation with Sam because she didn't want to upset him.

They went outside and got into the car. The game forecast called for cloudy skies and temperatures in the low fifties. In her indigo-blue skinny jeans, red scoop neck T-shirt and quilted jacket, she knew she would be warm for the ninety minutes of play.

She backed out of the driveway and headed toward the high school.

Josh turned in his seat. "What's going to happen to Sam when the season is over?"

Mariella shrugged and watched his smile disappear.

"He won't be hanging around anymore, right?"

She shook her head. "No. He's returning to London to become head coach of Emerald Premier."

"I wonder why he hasn't told the team."

She stole a glance at him. "He's probably waiting until after the playoffs to announce it."

Josh slumped against the seat, a look of defeat on his face. "I was kind of getting used to him working with me on soccer one-on-one."

"I know, and I've seen how your playing has improved."

"Plus, you've been happier, Mom."

She braked for a red light. "What are you trying to say, Josh?"

"If he makes you happy, Mom, I think you should be together. Don't you?"

"What are you doing, trying to get rid of me?"

Mariella eased the car forward and gave him a sideways glance. "You know, there was a time when you didn't want us together."

"I'm a kid, what do I know?" he joked. Then a look of regret crossed his face. "Mom, I'm sorry, but I was wrong about Sam."

Her mind was in a whirl as she pulled into the school parking lot, but she knew Josh deserved to know the whole story.

"There's a second part to Sam's new job. He wants me to come to England with him. I'd have to give up our home, my new job, and I'm not sure I'm willing to do that right now. More important, I'd also miss you too much."

"But, Mom, when will you have another chance to travel the world with someone you care about?"

Mariella turned off the ignition and opened her mouth to protest, but deep down she knew Josh was right.

"I'm going away to college. It's time for me to grow up and get used to being on my own. I can fly out to see you on college breaks."

He grabbed his bag, signifying the conversation must end soon. "I have my whole life ahead of me, and so do you. Give him a chance, Mom. Do what makes you happy."

The door slammed and sounded like a wake-up call. This time, her heart listened.

The season was officially over.

Mariella took a deep breath as she watched Sam finalize their late-night meal. She could not imagine what was going through his mind. The Titans had lost the game when the opposing team made a goal in the final minutes, and they would not be advancing in the playoffs.

Josh was out with the rest of the team, consoling themselves with burgers and shakes, and she was with the man she loved.

A man who would soon be leaving her.

She walked up to Sam and tapped on his shoulder. He turned around, the expression on his face cloaked in the dimness of the candlelit room.

"Thanks again for coming over," he said. "Under the circumstances, I wasn't sure if you would."

"I'm sorry about the loss tonight. I couldn't let you be alone."

"Josh played a good game. They all did." He glanced up at the ceiling, and then shook his head. "We almost had them, until that hat trick at the end."

"Easy come, easy go, right?" she said, trying to invoke some cheer into her voice.

He lowered his chin. "It's never easy to lose, Mariella."

"Do you regret taking the job?"

"No. I don't regret anything. Not anymore."

Sam searched her eyes, and she felt herself succumbing to the tender emotion she saw in them.

"Mariella, we've both chosen the path we think will work best for us."

"Even though it will tear us apart?" she asked.

He cupped her face in his hands, but didn't kiss her.

"You may not believe this, but I wish things didn't have to be this way."

She smiled, held back tears. "Your agent is too good at his job."

Sam laughed. "Niles is a pain in my rear sometimes, but he does try to get the best deal for me."

"No heart, all bankroll?"

"And damn the consequences," he added, crushing her to his muscular chest. "I felt bad about the way we ended things the other night."

"I'm glad I'm here," she said, playing with his tie as she looked into his eyes. "I couldn't stay away, Sam."

After a few moments, though she didn't really want to, she stepped away from his embrace.

"I also wanted to tell you how much meeting you has meant to Josh. He has really bloomed as a player, and as a person, under your tutelage."

He reached out and pressed his thumb against her lips, stirring her desire.

"And what about you?"

"I still can't kick a soccer ball." She poked him in the chest. "Because you never taught me."

Sam gave her a sad, mischievous smile and slapped his own hand. "I didn't? Shame on me."

Tears smarted in her eyes and she brushed them away. "Don't worry. You may still get the chance."

Smiling brightly, she continued, "I know you probably don't want to hear this right now, but I do have some good news. I heard earlier today that we got the grant for the new field."

He clapped his hands, but he still looked forlorn. "That's terrific. The Titans and the entire district will benefit from a new field. Too bad I won't be here to see the construction of it."

"They can send us pictures," she blurted before she lost her nerve.

Sam cupped his hand behind his ear. "Say again?"

Mariella took a deep breath. "I want to go with you to England, Sam. If you'll still have me."

He whooped loudly, gathered her into his arms and

twirled her about the room. Afterward, he gave her a long, passionate kiss.

"What made you change your mind? Wait, don't tell me yet." He started to pepper her neck with more kisses and she giggled and squirmed with happiness.

"Okay, now tell me."

When she finally had a chance to speak, her tone was serious. "That a life without you is no life at all."

"I was thinking the very same thing. Losing a soccer game is no match to losing the love of your life. That's why I was so sad tonight. The thought that we were about to share one last meal, that I'd never see you again. It was too much to bear."

She felt a tingle go down her spine at his words and she laid her cheek against his chest. She felt his heart beating, and knew she would always cherish him.

"Now, we never have to be apart."

He traced a finger along her jaw and then stroked his hand through her long hair. "I do have a bit of bad news, though."

Mariella's heart plummeted and she broke away. "What is it? Tell me! Though I'm not sure I can take it."

Her eyes widened with surprise when he dug into his pants pocket and brought out a large, glittery diamond ring.

"Remember when I ran into Josh at the mall on Christmas Eve? I had just come out of the jewelry store. I'd bought this, not knowing exactly what I would do with it at the time, especially since I had to guess your size. I'm hoping I got it right, but the jeweler said I could come back and get it resized any time at no extra charge."

She felt her excitement growing as she watched him fumble with, and then hold up the ring. He really appeared to be nervous, but his eyes were full of emotion.

"Mariella, I'm great at soccer, but I've never been good with words, and I'm just really worried about what you'll say."

"Just ask me, Sam," she begged, tears running down her cheeks.

As he got down on his good knee before her, she put her hands over her open mouth.

"Mariella, I love you more than any other woman I've ever known. Will you marry me?"

"Yes!"

He slipped the ring on her finger and it fit perfectly.

Mariella fell to her knees and wrapped her hands around his neck.

"I love you, Sam. Oh, I love you so much."

She gave the man of her dreams a tender kiss, grateful for his love, and a second chance at happiness.

Epilogue

"This is for you, Mr. and Mrs. Kelly."

The flight attendant set a small box tied with a red bow on the table in front of them, and left the couple alone.

Sam had hired a private jet to take them from Bay Point to London.

"It's from Ruby's!" Mariella exclaimed, pointing at the sticker with the shop's logo.

He kissed his new bride on her neck. "Well, open it up and see what it is."

She pushed him away playfully and untied the ribbon.

Inside there was a miniature wedding cake with white frosting, adorned with two silver bells.

"Oh, it's so beautiful!" Mariella exclaimed as she carefully lifted it out of the box.

He snapped a photo with her phone.

"There's a card, too," Mariella continued, smiling for the picture. "It says 'Congratulations on your wedding day.

Enjoy this little slice of home on your journey to your new life. Love, Leslie and the entire Bay Point High PTA.'"

"So, she does have a heart," Sam joked.

"Of course she does, and I hope her husband sees that once again someday."

"What do you mean?"

"Oh, it's nothing. Just remembering some girl talk."

Mariella sprung out of her seat. "I have something for you."

She disappeared into the sleeping compartment and emerged with a small box in her hand. She presented it to him, palms up. He kissed one and took the gift out of the other.

When he opened it, he felt his face flush warm with love. It was the smallest whistle he'd ever seen, in 14-karat gold on a gold chain.

"It's my wedding gift to you, and a congratulations for your new job."

"Thank you, Mariella. Put it on for me, please?"

She hung it around his neck and fastened the tiny clasp. When she was finished, he pulled her into his lap.

"I love it, and I love you. I'm sorry I had to be away for so long."

A week after proposing to her, Sam left for London to join the Emeralds as coach. He'd been gone for two months, traveling around Europe for games.

"I love you, too." She gave him a quick kiss on the lips. "Don't worry about the time away. It gave me time to get the house ready for renting. Josh had his senior prom, and then the whirlwind of graduation. Plus, I had a wedding to plan."

"The wedding was beautiful, wasn't it?"

"It was perfect," Mariella agreed.

She admired the bouquet of flowers that were an exact replica of the ones she'd carried down the aisle.

"Small and elaborate at the same time. I can't wait to see the feature on our nuptials in *Bay Point Living* magazine."

Josh, Emily, Leslie and her husband, Ida and Mr. Wexler attended. Mariella's parents did, too. Niles, Sam's agent, and a few of Sam's former teammates had also flown in for the nuptials.

Josh was going to spend a few weeks in Mexico with Emily and her family, while Ida and Mr. Wexler were headed up to Alaska on a buying trip. Sam didn't know what antiques they would find there, but maybe his mother would finally find love, and would be as happy as he was. After all, she had caught Mariella's bouquet.

"You're so gorgeous. I would have married you anywhere, even naked on the beach."

She laughed.

"Are you blushing?" Sam teased.

Mariella nodded. "Yes. I'm wondering why you're staring at me."

He winked. "To be honest, I was trying to figure out how I'm going to run interference on all those pearl buttons running down your back."

"It's easy. All you have to do is close your eyes."

"With pleasure."

She stood up, reached her arm behind her back and slipped down the zipper.

Sam heard the gown fall to the ground and hardened instantly.

"You can open up your eyes now."

He'd hardly been able to keep his hands off her on the limousine ride to the airport. But now, seeing his wife in a white lacy corset and garters with silk hose was unbelievably exciting.

"Love the high heels," he muttered hoarsely.

She ran her hands down the hose he'd brought her from London. "Mind if I keep them on?"

"Only if you'll let me take them off eventually."

He followed her into the sleeping compartment, shut

the door and tore down his pants as Mariella undid her hair from its updo style. It flowed around her shoulders and breasts in the most tantalizing way. He reached out to touch her, and she batted his hand away and began to slowly unbutton his shirt.

She laughed. "You forgot something."

He looked down and his tuxedo pants were puddled around his ankles, his shoes still on.

He couldn't bear to be away from her, even for a moment, he'd waited so long. So anxious to be with his bride, to feel her skin against his, and finally be one in body and heart, as a married couple.

"I'm trying, I'm trying."

He gritted his teeth, refusing to sit down on the bed and take off his shoes normally.

She snapped one of her garters against her thigh.

"Try faster."

Finally, he was free of his clothing. "Ready to join the mile-high club?"

She pressed her body to his and nodded. "But first, give me a kiss for good luck?"

He gathered her in his arms. "I've got something better in mind. How about a kiss that lasts forever?"

Winning Mariella's heart was only the first step, and he was thankful that he had his whole life to prove how much he loved her.

She pursed her lips against his ear. "What are we waiting for?"

"Not a thing."

He cradled her in his arms and laid her on the bed, his voice choked with emotion. "Not anymore."

* * * * *

KIMANI
ROMANCE™

COMING NEXT MONTH
Available November 20, 2018

#597 BACHELOR UNBOUND
Bachelors in Demand • by Brenda Jackson
International jeweler Zion Blackstone felt an instant connection to Celine Michaels. When she shows up at his house in Rome claiming kidnappers are after her, he offers the Hollywood producer's daughter his protection…and passion. But a revelation could upend his chance with Celine…

#598 A LOS ANGELES RENDEZVOUS
Millionaire Moguls • by Pamela Yaye
Jada Allen's Christmas wish list is simple: her gorgeous boss. A-list talent agent Max Moore counts on Jada to handle his life. Yet workaholic Max never notices her until a makeover reveals the woman he's taken for granted. Will one hot night shatter their working relationship or lead to something sweeter?

#599 ANOTHER CHANCE WITH YOU
The DuGrandpres of Charleston • by Jacquelin Thomas
Retired Secret Service agent Landon Trent stuns Jadin DuGrandpre with the announcement that they're still married. Winning back Jadin's trust won't be easy—especially when a trial pits the two Charleston attorneys on opposite sides. But Landon isn't giving up. Can they recapture what they once shared?

#600 HER MISTLETOE BACHELOR
Once Upon a Tiara • by Carolyn Hector
After a public breakup, CFO Donovan Ravens plans to spend the holidays alone in a small-town hotel. But science teacher British Carres has other ideas for the space the sexy bachelor booked. As they give in to their chemistry, a threat from the past could keep them from finding true love…

Get 4 FREE REWARDS!

We'll send you 2 FREE Books plus 2 FREE Mystery Gifts.

Harlequin® Desire books feature heroes who have it all: wealth, status, incredible good looks... everything but the right woman.

FREE Value Over **$20**

Her hands were shaking, but she grabbed her purse off the
mahogany table and forced a smile, one that concealed the anger
simmering inside her. "Max, you know what? You're right," she
said, nodding her head. "I'm a lowly administrative assistant. Who
am I to tell you what to do? Or advise you about how to parent your
daughter? I'm a nobody."

Max tried to interrupt her, to clarify what he'd said seconds
earlier, but Jada cut him off.

"*You* asked for my help, but the moment I disagreed with you you
decided my opinion was worthless, and now that I know how you
really feel about me, I can't work for you."

"You're twisting my words. I never said that."

"You didn't have to. I'm quite skilled at reading between the
lines…" Her voice wobbled, but she pushed past her emotions
and spoke in a self-assured tone. "I'll submit an official letter of
resignation first thing Monday, but consider this my two-week
notice."

Fear flashed in his eyes. "Jada, you can't quit. I need you. You're the heart and soul of Millennium Talent agency, and I'd be lost without you."

"Nonsense. You're the legendary Max Moore. One of the most revered talent agents in the city. You don't need me, or anyone else. You've got this, remember?"

Her mind made up, she turned and strode through the foyer.

Max slid in front of her, blocking her path. His cologne washed over her, and for a moment Jada forgot why she was mad at him. He licked his lips, and tingles flooded her body.

"You're quitting because I disagreed with you?" he asked, his eyebrows jammed together in a crooked line. "Because we argued about Taylor's outfit for her school dance?"

No, I'm quitting because I love you, and I'm tired of pretending I don't.

"Thanks for everything, Max. It was an honor to work for you. I've learned so much."

"I won't let you quit. We're a team, Jada, and I need you at the agency."

Scared her emotions would get the best of her, and she'd burst into tears if she spoke, Jada stepped past Max and yanked open the front door. He called out to her, but she didn't stop. Ignored his apologies. Increased her pace. Fleeing the million-dollar estate, with the feng shui fountain, the vibrant flower garden and the winding cobblestone driveway, she willed her heart not to fail, and her legs not to buckle.

Jada deactivated the alarm, slipped inside her car and started it. Anxious to leave, she put on her seat belt, then sped through the wrought-iron gates. In her rearview mirror, she spotted Max and his brothers standing on the driveway and wondered if they were discussing her dramatic exit. Jada dismissed the thought, told herself it didn't matter what the Moore brothers were doing. Max was her past, not her future, and she had to stop thinking about him. Gripping the steering wheel, Jada swallowed hard, blinking away the tears in her eyes.

Don't miss A Los Angeles Rendezvous
by Pamela Yaye, available December 2018
wherever Harlequin® Kimani Romance™
books and ebooks are sold.

Want to give in to temptation with steamy tales of irresistible desire?

Check out **Harlequin® Presents®**, **Harlequin® Desire** and **Harlequin® Kimani™ Romance** books!

CONNECT WITH US AT:

Facebook.com/groups/HarlequinConnection

 Facebook.com/HarlequinBooks

 Twitter.com/HarlequinBooks

 Instagram.com/HarlequinBooks

 Pinterest.com/HarlequinBooks

ReaderService.com